Jared looked at Melanie, and saw the flushed face wet from crying, the star-blue eyes looking at him in pleading and trust. **Help me.**

Resent her as he had for taking Anna's focus from their marriage, taking her love from him, never in his life had Jared been able to resist a cry for help. Anna deserved the rest, and Melanie was so little, so helpless....

He gathered her up, grabbed a clean bottle, a spare diaper and cleaning stuff from the bag, and slipped back outside the door, closing it behind him. He carried her through to the kitchen, and automatically filled the kettle with water for a bottle—and a coffee. "Now what's wrong, little one?" he asked softly as he jiggled her on his shoulder.

OUTBACK *Baby Tales*

Newborns, new arrivals, newlyweds

In a beautiful but isolated landscape, three sisters
follow three very different routes to parenthood
against all odds and find love with brooding men....

Discover the soft side of these rugged cattlemen
as they win over feisty women
and a handful of adorable babies!

Your journey through the tears and triumphs
begins here:

One Small Miracle
by Melissa James
Available April 2010

The Cattleman, the Baby and Me
by Michelle Douglas
Available May 2010

**And the pitter-patter of tiny feet continues
with *Their Newborn Gift*
by Nikki Logan**
Available June 2010

MELISSA JAMES
One Small Miracle

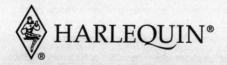

TORONTO • NEW YORK • LONDON
AMSTERDAM • PARIS • SYDNEY • HAMBURG
STOCKHOLM • ATHENS • TOKYO • MILAN • MADRID
PRAGUE • WARSAW • BUDAPEST • AUCKLAND

Recycling programs
for this product may
not exist in your area.

ISBN-13: 978-0-373-74021-5

ONE SMALL MIRACLE

First North American Publication 2010

Copyright © 2010 by Lisa Chaplin

Melissa James is a mother of three, living in a beach suburb in New South Wales, Australia. A former nurse, waitress, shop assistant, perfume and chocolate demonstrator—among other things—she believes in taking on new jobs for the fun experience. She'll try anything at least once, to see what it feels like—a fact that scares her family on regular occasions. She fell into writing by accident, when her husband brought home an article stating how much a famous romance author earned, and she thought, *I can do that!* She can be found most mornings walking and swimming at her local beach with her husband, or every afternoon running around to her kids' sporting hobbies, while dreaming of flying, scuba diving, belaying down a cave or over a cliff—anywhere her characters are at the time!

To Vicky, who taught all who knew her
about bearing sudden life change with dignity,
courage and grace. We'll always miss you.

CHAPTER ONE

Broome, North-Western Australia

ALL day the heat had been like a headache, pulsing and thick with moisture. The local Aboriginal clans called this 'knock-'em-down' season—the clouds were a dark-and-brilliant tapestry covering the sky, and the rumbling thunder, lightning forking across the beach, brought the entire landscape to fascinating, terrifying life. Then at last the wild storms came, the unrelenting rain fell, cutting off the entire Kimberley region from the rest of the world, apart from a few brave souls that ventured here on the one highway that stayed open. The shops all closed in the town from just after New Year to the start of February, apart from grocery and the petrol stations, the resorts and the odd souvenir store.

Her little grocery/souvenir shop stayed open for those few tourists who came in. It opened at seven a.m., and stayed open until seven at night. She had to fill her life with something, right?

Anna West—soon to be Curran once again—walked along the beach toward the small apartment she'd taken five months ago. Cable Beach was her favourite place in the world. Dazzling creamy-white sands were littered with rocks and stunning aqua water, and sometimes, not as often as the famed Monkey Mia beach, but sometimes the dolphins came so close to the shore you could pat them, and the whales swam past on a journey to and from the Antarctic, leaping from the crystalline water to give tantalising glimpses of long, sleek, grey beauty, their family lives evident in their care for their little ones…

Don't think about it, not on this of all days.

She wiped the sweat running down her face and kept walking, her eyes blinded to the beauty. She'd look again tomorrow, love it then as she always had. Not today. One year since—

Anna knew she shouldn't be alone today. She had plenty of places to go, if she wanted to.

'Come to Perth, Anna. You can stay with me as long as you want to. You'll have total peace and quiet here—but you won't be alone,' Sapphie told her during every call, in that gentle yet insistent way of hers. Sapphie, her long-time best friend from their boarding-school days, the daughter of

Jarndirri's former housekeeper, would never give up until Anna came.

'Come to Yurraji, Anna,' her sister, Lea, would say. 'You don't need to run that stupid shop—Broome's got twenty of them already—but you've only got one niece. Molly needs to see her only aunt—and you should be with your family now.'

Anna knew that beneath Lea's gruff, commanding tone—so much like their dad's—was a world of anxiety she felt for her little sister. She could never say 'I love you, I miss you', and especially not 'I'm scared for you'. Lea was a fighter, not a lover—but it was in every call, in every unspoken word.

Yurraji was the property Granddad had left Lea. It lay in the wildest, most remote part of Western Australia where brumbies, the wild horses, still ran free, and Lea could gentle them and give them a sanctuary. Anna could spend a week, a month or whatever she needed—and she'd never find a place more peaceful, or farther away from gossip and speculation.

Both Lea and Sapphie called every evening to check on her, as they'd done for the past year, bearing with her monosyllabic replies with more patience and love than she had a right to expect. Their calls made the long, lonely evenings bearable, and yet…

The bitter cocktail sloughed down her throat

again, the shame and resentment of her own sister, her dearest friend—but the worst was that she couldn't even bear to talk to her only, adored niece. Hanging up the phone when she heard Molly's little, piping voice cry, 'I wanna talk Aunty Anna!'

She'd do it—soon. One day. When even hearing Molly's voice didn't set off images…

Images of Molly playing with her baby cousin… Lea, Sapphie and Molly exclaiming over Adam's first tooth, his first smile, his first steps while she and Jared almost burst with pride over every word, Adam's every achievement.

The rain was falling again, and not from the sky.

Anna swiped savagely at her treacherous eyes. *Stop it. Just don't think about it.*

It was her daily mantra. As if she repeated it often enough, something might happen—perhaps a convenient dose of amnesia, or she'd wake up beside Jared fifteen months ago. She'd pull his hand over her enormous mound of belly, and they'd smile together as a little hand or foot travelled across, as if waving. *Hi, Mummy, Daddy…*

A dark *boom* of thunder sounded from over the ocean, coming in ripples across the water. She broke into a run, heading across the sand to the end of the lane connecting the beach and the main street, where her little house sat in wonky pride.

A shabby cottage with a sagging verandah, built to face the waves at the side of the beach, did her just fine. She didn't need the big, gleaming apartment in the centre of town that Jared had bought for her, as befitted a Curran. Her cottage was private, and that was all she wanted.

As she passed, the wafting scent of the local takeaway-cum-anything shop enticed her. She'd stop and grab some fish and chips, take them home and grab a DVD. Maybe Monty Python... nobody could feel self-pity while they watched Monty Python. She'd smile and laugh and almost forget for an hour or two.

Half an hour later she let herself in her door, munching on the chips she'd bought through a hole she'd punched in the top of the paper wrapping. She plopped the stuff down on the coffee table, opened the DVD and pushed it into the player, grabbing the remote—

A loud, aggressive knock on her door startled her from pushing the *on* button.

Jared.

She stiffened her spine. She'd handed him a million prime Kimberley hectares on a platter when she'd walked out five months before. Why did he keep trying to bring her back? *Because he's the kind of man who doesn't know how to lose.* He'd made a pact with her father: if he married her, he'd inherit Jarndirri, and The Great Outback Legend Jared

West could never be seen to welch on a deal. It would humiliate him in front of all his peers almost as much as his wife daring to leave him.

The knock this time was imperative, harder than the thunder crashing overhead.

Anna called, 'Coming!', and, gritting her teeth, walked to the door without rushing. She couldn't seem eager to see him or he'd know he could take advantage. A single kiss and she'd be gone. Heaven knew how hard it had been the first few times. He'd had her stripped half-naked and melting in a puddle at his feet before she'd regained her senses, and thrown him out. She might not love him any more, but her body didn't seem to know the difference. One look at his face and the inner screaming for release began; one touch and all she could think about was him.

No more. It's over!

She threw open the door, her face lifted, ready to do battle—

But no six-two of rugged, dark-haired, dusty male filled the aperture. Instead was a young woman with a pretty face, a too-thin body, and desperate eyes pleading for help. 'Hi, Anna, um, hi, how are you…?'

Anna's heart didn't sink, it whacked her feet with its mile-a-second descent; yet the aching hunger came. She knew what Rosie Foster was about to ask, and she could no more deny her than she could stop breathing. 'I'm fine, Rosie. How are you and our beautiful Melanie today?'

Rosie jiggled the baby car seat in her hand as if in instinctive comfort. 'Um, we're good. Look, I know I have no right to ask you…'

The familiar terror and pain and hunger washed through Anna as she forced a smile to her face. Her only real friend in town, Rosie Foster never asked Anna about her life. She had enough troubles of her own. Rosie was a new mother, a single mother whose deadbeat ex had done a runner. She needed help, and had chosen Anna as her confidante and babysitter—probably *because* Anna never volunteered her own troubles in return. She had a constant listener and someone who'd never turn down the opportunity to mind her baby when Rosie needed a break.

Why me, Rosie? I can't do this again, I can't! Why had Rosie chosen her, barren Anna West, who'd lost her son and her womb in a day, and then walked out on the marriage that was almost a folk tale among the locals?

Maybe it was because Anna was even more fiercely alone than Rosie was. At least Rosie knew how to reach out, to ask for help; Anna didn't know how to lower her pride. Everyone hereabouts might know she'd walked out on Jared— and they all had their theories why—but she refused to indulge their curiosity, or their spite, by giving them a version of events, or sharing her most private anguish. She hadn't talked to anyone in a year. A year to this day…

Unable to stop herself, she dropped her gaze. A flushed, chubby face looked back up at her from the midst of a car seat, with big blue eyes and long golden lashes surrounded by a pink, frilly bonnet. Dimples peeped as a trusting smile filled the little face, sure of her welcome.

Hi, Aunty Anna, the beautiful eyes said without words. *I've come to play again… A* chubby little fist left a rosebud mouth; a tiny hand reached for her, the toothless little mouth smiled up at her in a drooling, adorable hello.

And Anna's heart, frozen for a long year—from the moment she'd known her beautiful boy was dying inside her and there was nothing she could do to save him—melted once again. 'Of course, Rosie, come on in, both of you. I've got dinner to share.'

It was almost time for the Wet again.

The clouds closed in every day, heavy as fleece bales after shearing, thick and dark and tinged with flecks of scarlet like blood. This time of year the clouds dominated the horizon from sunrise to sunset, moments of violent colour after dark, and before dark fell again. As if it had vanished, the sky wasn't there.

Just like Anna. He'd come home from feeding

the animals one hot afternoon five long months ago, calling for his wife—and had heard only his own echoes mocking him.

For the thousandth time, Jared West had re-read the note she'd left.

We both know it's over. I can't give you the chil-dren you want, and I can't stand living here any more—always alone, enduring the silence.

I don't need anything from the Jarndirri account. I have my mother's legacy. It's enough to live on. Use the money to run the place—it was always more yours than mine. Don't try to find me. I won't come back. Just accept this is a fence that can't be mended.

I'll file for divorce when the year's up. You can still have the children you want. It's not too late for you. Be happy.

That was it. A few scribbled lines with no name, hers or his. As if five years of marriage had meant nothing to her. It was as if all those years of making a home, working together through the harsh climate, fighting for the right to create a family, *their family*, had never existed for her.

So why couldn't he toss the stupid thing out? Anna had left him five months ago, never once tried to contact him, and threw him out every time he went to her little house on the edge of

Broome township—he knew from the first moment she'd go there; she loved the place. She'd even wanted to go there for their honeymoon instead of the six weeks in Europe he'd booked. He'd always promised to take her there for a week—one day.

Well, she had her way at last.

Last time he'd flown down to Broome, she hadn't even let him in the door. She'd handed him signed papers of legal separation, and said, 'Leave me alone, Jared. If you bother me again I'll file a restraining order.' Her eyes, soft, light brown and as gentle as a doe's in a sweet pixie face, had been filled with inflexible resolution. Then she'd closed the door in his face.

But how could he accept it was over when he didn't know *why*? Her note might as well be gibberish for all the sense it made. They'd had a fantastic life together, and they could have everything they'd lost—happiness, Jarndirri, and kids. He had it all planned out. He just had to bring her home.

When Adam had died…*his beautiful son*…he'd wanted to die too. But when Anna had woken up from the operation to the news that her uterus had split beyond repair—the cause of Adam's death, and her collapse within hours—and she'd had an emergency hysterectomy, his loving, perfect wife had gone away. She'd turned from everyone close to her, especially him and Lea. Sapphie, the only one she talked to, wouldn't tell him what Anna was saying or feeling.

'Ask her yourself, Jared,' was all she said. 'Talk to her.'

But Anna refused to talk to him. He understood how hard it was on her, but he refused to give up hope. After months of research, he'd found a way for them to have the kids they longed for. He had it all planned. He'd been waiting for her to heal before he brought it up.

But despite everything he'd tried, Anna hadn't healed. She'd walked out on him, on their life—on everything.

Everything felt wrong without Anna. No matter what was stated on the deed of ownership, Anna was The Curran, the fourth generation of the Curran dynasty on Jarndirri. Without her he felt as if he was fumbling around the station, working at all that was familiar and loved in darkness so dense he couldn't see through it. He felt like an interloper in the only life he'd always wanted, the only dream he'd ever had.

Without Anna, he was nothing but a fraud—just as his father had been—

Don't go there. But every day since she'd left, he seemed to have lost control even over his mind. The memory came day and night…

Jared shuddered. At fourteen, he'd had the last day of his childhood—and his last day as a West.

He'd become a Curran even before the funeral. It seemed his mother couldn't give him away fast enough—but at least she'd given him to the Currans.

In a world where one wrong word could tear his world apart, the Currans had made everything right. He'd lost his father, but in Bryce Curran he'd found a strong working man of the land, a man in whom he could be proud to be called son. He'd lost his brothers and sisters, but in Lea he'd had the straight-talking, gruffly affectionate sister of his heart.

And in Anna…he'd found his destiny.

Anna made his life *work*. With a smile, a touch, she banished the ugly demons to the furthest corner of his mind. With Anna by his side he was The Curran, the man chosen to continue the proud traditions of the famed Jarndirri clan. He was strong, he could do anything.

But now she was gone, who was he? What was he?

He folded the letter, returning it to his pocket. It was almost nightfall; there were another fifteen jobs to do before Mrs Button would serve the dinner. So why was he hanging around the house, an hour before he needed to?

There was only one answer—he was waiting to hear the phone ring, on this of all days. It would have been Adam's first birthday today. God help him, he could *see* his son's face as he crawled or toddled after him—swinging Adam on his hip, putting him on his first pony or patting the cows…

He *needed* Anna to come home. She had to come back to him. Jarndirri was their heart and soul. They'd first kissed here, become engaged here, even married here. And this hour before sunset had always been 'their' time of the day, when they'd worked together, talked before dinner—or made love in the shower.

A gravelled curse tore from his throat. He slammed his Akubra on his head, and strode out the door. His personal ghost followed him with soft words his straining ears could almost hear.

'Dinner's in an hour, Jared. Can I help you with anything? Or is it time for a shower? You do look…sweaty,' she'd say, with that sweet, naughty smile of hers.

'Stop haunting me,' he muttered as he stalked down the stairs, flung himself onto his motorbike and revved it up hard. The men were at dinner. He wouldn't call for help he didn't need. There were no actual fences on Jarndirri, like every other property in the Kimberley—how could you fence a single property that was the size of the whole of modern London?—but he needed to make sure the cattle were close to the few fenced-in paddocks, safe within the unseen bounds of his kingdom. The wide-wandering livestock had to be made secure before the bucketing-down rain came, any day, any hour now, and the creeks became rivers, the rivers became torrential seas and valuable animals were caught in the swelling waters and drowned.

'Mr West, Mr West!'

He called to the cook-housekeeper, 'What is it, Ellie?' He kept his tone neutral. It wasn't her fault her voice grated on him. Any woman's voice but Anna's did that these days. Even Lea's voice got to him…*especially* Lea's voice. It wasn't fair, he knew; she was trying so hard to be fair to them both; but he could barely stand being civil. She sounded so much like—

He blinked and wheeled around, facing Ellie Button. 'What did you say?' The engine must be running too loud, or he was hallucinating. He couldn't have heard—

'Mrs West is on the phone. She needs to talk to you. It sounds—urgent.'

An hour later

'Hell, Jared, this isn't a joke! You're flying fifty knots over the legal limit. You might be the best pilot in the Kimberleys, but there's laws for a reason. You gotta slow down, mate, or you'll kill yourself!'

When Jared ignored the frantic yells of one of four local air traffic controllers in the region, Tom growled, 'Right, that's it. I've cleared the airspace around you so you don't kill anyone else—but I'm callin' Bill, and lettin' him deal with you when you get into Broome. But don't hit the tower 'cause I'm in it, and if I survive I'll kill you myself!'

Bring it on. Jared grinned in pure challenge. Nothing short of that lightning strike was stopping him from getting to Broome, to Anna. He knew Tom was right—the first storm of the season was about to hit, and he was flying right into the danger zone. But after five long, empty months Anna had called him at last. After a year of waiting, she'd finally sounded *alive*, and he was bringing her home before she changed her mind.

'Right-oh, Jared, you want to be an idiot? You want trouble, mate, you got it,' Tom screamed. 'Bill'll be waitin' for you at the airport. You're doin' a night in lock-up, and facin' multiple charges, unless you slow down right now!'

Jared grinned again, and messaged the car rental company, asking them to bring the car to the less-used airstrip for the resort people. He'd cop a fine for that too, but it was closer to Anna's place. Hopefully he'd get there before Bill caught him.

Forty minutes later, he landed the plane hard and fast. Though he'd changed direction at the last possible moment, Tom would have followed his flight pattern, cottoned onto his plan, and had probably sent Bill on his way here. Jared headed down the tarmac toward the hangar, pulling off to the side as close as possible to where the car waited. He tossed a huge tarpaulin cover over the plane for protection, threw a thousand in cash at the stunned driver and said, 'I'll leave the keys in the car back here tomorrow. Keep the change.'

And he took off in a roar of dirt, ignoring the man's bewildered cry, 'But how do I get back to town?' It would only take someone five minutes to come and get him.

He'd been on the road all of three minutes when the expected siren began wailing behind him. When Bill circled around him to block off escape and pulled him over to the side of the road, Jared wound down the window, said, 'You know my address, Bill. Send me the tickets and charges,' and screeched back onto the road while Bill bolted back to the police van.

He kept driving over the limit while Bill followed him, lights flashing and siren wailing, all the way to Anna's. He didn't care how much he had to pay. All he could think was that, if he let Bill take him in, he'd be away for hours, and Anna would change her mind.

'Something's happened. I need to see you, Jared—as soon as you can,' she'd said tentatively, as if expecting him to say no. Yet there was something else there, too—something besides the gut-wrenching numbness, which was all he'd known from her for the past year. 'Can you come tonight?'

'I'll be there in two hours,' was all he'd said.

And he would be. Anna was coming home tonight. He wasn't allowing for any chance of failure. Whatever she wanted, she could have; whatever she needed, she'd get. Whatever it took to bring her home, he'd do it. She was the queen of Jarndirri, she was the Curran—she was his *wife*. She belonged with him.

He arrived at her door, read the note, pulled it off the door and knocked softly, as instructed. He didn't know why, and didn't care. She'd called him, she wanted to see him at last, and that was all that mattered. The rest he could make right. He'd find the way.

She opened the door with a half-smile, tentative, even insecure. Her reddish-brown hair with stripy golden bits, like half-cooked toffee, was pulled back in a messy ponytail with tendrils sticking out everywhere. She had sweat running down her flushed face; there was a glob of something white on her cheek. Her black-lashed doe eyes held fear and welcome and—

Then her gaze swivelled to the right, and her eyes widened. 'Why is Bill chasing you?'

He couldn't answer. She was messy, she was adorable, she was Anna and he was starving for her. He pulled her into his arms and kissed her, deep and drugging, before she could say a word. He wasn't giving her a chance to say no. He had to touch her, imprint her taste on him again. A streak ran through him, a brilliant connection of synapses to senses to skin, and he was *alive* for the first time in weeks.

He heard her tiny moan, the soft sound of surrender to the passion that flared between them so easily, as her hands touched his chest. Then she pushed him away. 'Stop it. That's not why I asked you to come.' Then her cheeks became suffused with colour as Bill strode up the path, his face filled with inflexible duty. 'Why is Bill here?' she whispered.

He barely heard her first words. *My Golden Girl*, he thought, with a shot of exultation. *She always has to be a lady.* Even mucking out a stall in grubby overalls or breaking in a young colt, riding with dirty, bare feet, she wouldn't kiss him if anyone was around.

'To give me about twenty tickets,' he muttered, feeling like the most stupid jerk in the Kimberley region. Remembering too late how much she hated public displays of any kind.

Bill caught up to him at last. 'Jared West, you're under arrest for the violation of at least seventeen laws, including speeding, resisting arrest—'

Jared's agonised glance at Anna shocked him. She showed neither embarrassment nor exasperation now, but wide-eyed terror. 'Get rid of him.' She hauled him close to whisper in his ear as Bill read him his rights. 'Please, Jared.' She sounded frantic. 'He'll ruin everything!'

He didn't have time to question it. Anna had few wants, and had never begged him for anything before, ever. This weird request had to be really important. So he put out his wrists. 'Take me.' As Bill put the cuffs on him, he swivelled his head to face her. 'I'll be back.'

'Not tonight, you won't,' Bill said in grim promise, and led him away. 'Anna, you know where to come to bail him out in the morning. If you decide you want to.'

Watching her as he stumbled after Bill, Jared saw her cheeks drain to white. 'Jared, I—I'm sorry,' she called. 'I can't bail you just yet. I'll come tomorrow.'

He felt his brows lift. Whatever Bill thought, he'd assumed that, since he'd just become a felon for her sake, she'd follow and pay the bail.

Something was definitely weird here and, whatever it was, he'd discover it soon enough... after he'd spent the night in the slammer.

CHAPTER TWO

Broome Police Station, next morning

'YOU know I wouldn't cheat you. It's all there. I'm kind of in a hurry, Bill. Can I take my husband home now, please?'

From the holding cell, sitting on the thin mattress on a squeaky metal base that passed for a bed, Jared felt his brows lift. He didn't care why she wanted him out so fast after leaving him here all night, and not coming in until eleven in the morning. He'd slept on the ground during muster too many times to care about an almost-dead mattress in the local lock-up. But he *was* going to find out why his conservative wife had been so desperate to get rid of Bill yesterday, why she'd taken his arrest without a blink.

'You're sure you want to?' Bill asked, low, with a strangely intimate note, man to woman—and Jared clenched his fists.

'I wouldn't be here if I wasn't sure. Please, can you let him out now?'

Too slowly for Jared's taste, Bill unlocked the cell. The young cop nodded back toward Anna, with a meaning frown. 'She's a real lady,' he said quietly. 'You're lucky she's here at all after your stupid stunts yesterday. She deserves better than that. You need to stop taking tomfool chances with your life. Take better care of her, Jared. She's…special.'

Defensive, possessive, he was about to retort, *I always take care of her*—then he remembered the one incident of deadly neglect of his wife he'd never forgive himself for; knew everyone in the Kimberleys knew of it. Then he wondered what would have happened to her if he'd killed himself in his speeding efforts yesterday…and he remembered how Bill, a young, good-looking single guy sent out here after academy eight years ago, had been looking at Anna yesterday and this morning, counting the cash slowly and making conversation.

And he remembered how long she'd been alone. *Back off, jerk. She's mine.* He felt his fists curl over…and he saw Bill noticing. The cop's chin lifted with a little smile, as if begging for him to start, to toss the first punch.

He wasn't giving Bill any further advantage by acting stupid. He gave a nod and pushed past the cop, striding over to where Anna waited. She was neatly dressed now in long creamy shorts and a pink tank top, her hair loose and falling straight to her shoulder blades, and so subtly sensual, so fresh and elfin-pretty, he had to fight against hauling her into his arms in a display of primal possession.

Instead he gave her the slow half-smile she'd never been able to resist. It was time to start playing smart. And for a single moment she looked at him as if he was her salvation.

He thought, *Mission accomplished, she's coming home*—but then he saw her fingers twisting around each other in subtle anxiety. 'Oh, please hurry. We have to get back now.'

He still had to sign the form that said he'd show up to court at a set date, and collect his things— Bill had taken his watch and wedding ring as scrupulously as if he'd been a real criminal—and by then Anna was twitching her toes, lacing and unlacing her fingers.

She all but dragged him out of the police station, with a rushed, polite 'Bye, Bill' that told Jared the attraction was one-sided—and that shot of triumphant, primal masculine ownership streaked through him again. At least that was one worry to tick off his list. He was another step closer to bringing her home. She was finally *feeling* again. She'd crawled out of that black hole of despair she'd fallen into. And once she was home, he could tell her the plans he'd made for their family, make her smile and laugh again...

They'd reached the car, and she jumped into the

driver's seat with a fierce look that dared him to argue. 'We have to get back right now. The train goes in an hour and—'

'What train? What's going on, Anna?' he growled. If she thought she was leaving—

She talked right over him. 'We need to make sure she gets on the train—Rosie, my friend Rosie Foster. She needs our help, Jared—both of us.'

'Who's Rosie Foster, and what does she want with me?' *What do you want with me?*

'I told you, she's my friend, and she needs help.'

'Why me? Why now?' The curiosity gnawed at him. 'You didn't want to know me a few days ago when I called, and now you'll do anything for me—except bail me out last night,' he added, angling for a laugh from her, or even a smile. She seemed so anxious.

She kept driving without looking at him. Her whole focus was on the road. 'Just wait until we're at my place. Then you'll see.'

No adorable, naughty smile. No soft voice filled with yearning. She was barely listening to him, and hadn't touched him since dragging him out to the car, which barely qualified. And now, hours too late, he heard the words she'd said yesterday when he'd kissed her.

That's not why I asked you to come.

Whatever she wanted him for, it didn't seem to be about coming back to him.

Failure wasn't an option, now she'd called at last. She was coming home. She'd forgotten how much she loved their home, how much she needed and loved him—but he'd remind her.

Forcing a semblance of calm, Jared sat back and waited. For the first time in their twelve-year relationship he had to allow Anna to take the driver's seat. He'd let her keep control for now, until he knew who this Rosie was, what she needed—and what the real story was here.

He'd formulate a plan in the interim. Whatever waited for them at her house, he'd use it to his advantage. He'd make her come home, and then, no matter what it took, no matter the cost, he'd win her back to him. She'd adored him once; she'd loved their life on Jarndirri as much as he had. He'd resurrect both those loves, and take his life back.

He'd make it happen.

Anna's hands were shaking with worry by the time she opened the door—Rosie was terrified about the step she needed to take, and the possible repercussions—but the quiet within the house reassured her. Rosie must have taken a nap, as well.

She drew in a breath of relief, and moved aside to let Jared in. 'Come in and sit down. I'll put the kettle on and make coffee in a minute.' She ran into her bedroom to check on the baby.

In the middle of the big queen bed, surrounded by every chair in the house, carefully wrapped in a blanket, Melanie lay sleeping peacefully in the bassinette Rosie had brought. Melanie's cheeks were flushed pretty pink in the humidity; her fingers were curled around her nose as she sucked her thumb. Her bare toes twitched.

Anna's heart filled with relief, and overflowed with joy. She couldn't resist... She crept over to the bed and whisper-caressed the pudgy cheek, warm and pretty pink. 'Hello, beautiful girl, I'm back,' she murmured. 'Did you wear your poor mummy out?' The word jerked in her heart. Such a beautiful word, *mummy*, so taken for granted...

'What the *hell*...?'

The explosive words from the doorway made the baby start, and give a tiny wail. She sounded tired, querulous. 'Be quiet,' Anna whispered frantically, soothing the baby with gentle touches. 'She's only been asleep an hour.'

After a moment's protest, Melanie's eyes closed, her thumb went farther into her mouth and she drifted back to dreamland.

White-faced and dark-eyed, like a cloud filled with unleashed thunder, Jared barked from the doorway, 'Whose baby is that? Where did you...?'

The kettle began whistling. Frantic to keep the place quiet for the baby, she shoved at his chest and pushed him right out the door, and closed it silently behind her. 'Get into the kitchen, *now*.'

The menace was about to unleash. He stalked to the tiny, functional room, and pulled the kettle from the gas. When he turned to her, his face was even paler, his stormy eyes almost as black as the turbulent clouds outside. 'Anna, tell me what that baby's doing in your bed and who it belongs to.'

'Not *it*, she,' Anna corrected, pulling the coffee down from the cupboard with unsteady hands. She couldn't face him as she spooned grounds into the plunger.

If anything, his voice grew darker at her correction. 'Is this the Rosie you talked about? If so, you're insane. You can't put a kid that age on a train.'

She resisted the urge to roll her eyes. 'I might not know much, but I know that, Jared. Her name's Melanie. Rosie's her mother.'

'Okay, *she*,' he amended, still grim. 'Where is this Rosie, *who* is she, and why is her kid here?'

'We don't have time for this,' she said, pulling out mugs as an excuse to keep her eyes averted. 'We have to get Rosie on the train, and take Melanie to Jarndirri—'

Jared interrupted, with ruthless ice. 'I'm not doing a thing but going straight back to Bill to contact Child Services unless I find out exactly what's going on here.'

She felt the blood drain from her cheeks. 'You can't do that!'

'Watch me,' he said grimly, with a suspicion she'd never heard from Jared in all the years they'd known each other. 'I don't know what's going on here, but I doubt it's legal.'

Her mind blanked out. 'I…um, it's not illegal.'

He grabbed her arm, swung her around to him. His face was right in front of hers, his eyes blazing in disbelief. 'Dear God, Anna, did you kidnap that baby? Are you so desperate for a child you'd steal someone else's? Why didn't you *talk* to me? If I'd known— I have a solution for us—'

She felt the colour drain from her face at the questions she'd never thought he'd ask. 'How could you even think I'd—I'd do that…' she couldn't bring herself to say the word 'kidnap' '…knowing how I've been since we lost Adam? Do you think I could put another set of parents through the loss we endured?' She said it almost as indignantly as if he hadn't read her mind every time she'd seen a little boy or girl Adam's age in the past few months and put an unerring finger on the pulse of her secret shame. Because, oh, if she could get away with it…to hold a precious baby in her arms, to have chubby arms around her neck, to watch it grow, and hear it calling her Mummy…

He sighed and released her arms. 'Thank God,' he muttered, wiping at his brow. She saw the beads of sweat there, and she knew it hadn't been caused by the heat.

'You honestly think I could be capable of such an act?' she shot at him, but her voice wobbled. *Guilt, shame, passion, craving, loneliness…*

Why couldn't I just say yes to Rosie's impassioned proposal of last night? If I had, right now I'd have all I'd ever dreamed of…

'After a night in the slammer, and you desperate to get rid of Bill, it wasn't a big leap in logic once I saw the kid.' He paced over to the back door and opened it, breathing in a silence of relief, fear released. 'So whose baby is she?'

She gulped down the pain; her hands fluttered up. 'I told you, she's Rosie's child—and she needs our help for a few weeks.'

'Right, got it. So where is this mysterious Rosie?' he queried dryly. 'And *who* is she?'

'Rosie Foster. You remember her, Maggie Foster's girl? She grew up here, but left for university two or three years back.' Anna sighed when he shrugged; she was sure he did know, because everyone knew everyone else here. The Kimberleys might be bigger than France, but had a population about the size of Liechtenstein. 'She's asleep in the spare room, I guess, or packing. She's heading to Perth today. I— She's got postnatal depression, and nobody to turn to. We've become good friends in the past few months. She asked me to take Melanie for a few weeks while she gets help.'

Jared frowned again. 'Hang on. That makes no sense. Those places take the mother and child. Why isn't she taking the kid with her?'

'Melanie. *Her name is Melanie,*' Anna repeated with icy patience, but Jared merely shrugged, waiting for her to answer. 'Look, we can talk about this in the plane to Jarndirri, and, first, Rosie needs to get to the station. There's just one train going to Perth this week, and it leaves today…'

'No,' he replied, with a quiet inflexibility that told her this wasn't up for negotiation. He wasn't taking her anywhere until he had the details. 'That kid is not coming to Jarndirri. I'm already facing court for your sake, Anna. I won't be an accessory to kidnapping a child—and in the eyes of the law, that's what taking her to Jarndirri would be. Taking her one step out of this house without calling the cops means serious prison time—and it looks to me like Bill would love any excuse to lock me away, at least,' he added with a penetrating look.

Anna felt herself flushing, feeling almost as guilty as if she'd accepted any of Bill's many offers to have dinner, coffee or watch a DVD together. 'I didn't ask you to break any laws in getting here,' she snapped, exasperated and uncomfortably aware that her pleading tone over the phone had been its own request to a take-charge kind of man like Jared. 'I haven't broken any laws either. Taking Melanie to Jarndirri in no way constitutes…abduction. We have the mother's written permission to look after her for a few weeks.'

'Will you just tell me how the kid got here?' He spoke with a frown, with an exaggerated kind of patience that made her flush—and stop beating around the bush. She answered him in a crisp, cool voice that hid her defensiveness.

'Rosie came to me last night. She's been struggling to cope since she had the baby. But she's just been diagnosed with postnatal depression. She wants me to mind Melanie for a few weeks while she gets help.'

'Hasn't she got any family?' Now the tone was leashed; she felt the impatience straining from him. Wanting to know why—and what it had to do with him—but he must have picked up on her reluctance to tell the story all at once. Felt her longing to run, hard and fast, at the same time she yearned to look after a baby, even if it would never be her own.

'Her ex-boyfriend disappeared when she began showing, told her he had a wife and kids he'd already left. He didn't like being a father. He'd hooked up with her because she was a medical student, and wouldn't want kids for years. And her mother—remember Maggie?' she repeated with emphasis.

'Yes. What about her?'

Anna gritted her teeth, hearing that exaggerated patience again, the reluctance in listening, wanting her to get to the point. To Jared a story was just a vehicle to him finding the solution, and drawing it out with unnecessary hesitation or embellishment was useless.

Just as well I didn't want to become a writer, she thought wryly, before she answered. 'Rosie doesn't remember her father, and you know how Maggie was so intensely proud of Rosie being at university and becoming a doctor. She hates that Rosie chose to give up her medical studies and come home to have the baby. She threw her out and though she only lives an hour from here, she hasn't even seen Melanie. If Rosie leaves Melanie with Maggie, she's afraid the mother will use her depression as an excuse to get Child Services involved, or try to put the baby up for adoption.'

'Nice woman,' was his only comment, with a world of dryness. Hiding what they were both thinking. *Some people would give anything to have a beautiful, healthy baby, and she only sees it as a hindrance...*

'The train leaves in forty minutes. I need to wake Rosie right now if she's going to make it. The point is, Rosie wants me to take the baby to

Jarndirri for the few weeks she's gone—away from her mother's influence, and interference by the ex if he knew,' she said in a rush. 'We don't have much time. Will you do it?'

He looked at her for a long time, and Anna wanted to squirm. After all these months of him coming here, demanding she return home or seducing her into it, she'd thought—hoped—

'Go wake her. I'll meet her and make up my mind,' was all he said. His face was expressionless as always, and she wished for the hundredth time that she could see or feel anything from him—anything at all. That he could actually talk to her and say anything so she'd *know* this enigma she'd lived beside for half her life, the husband she still didn't know.

Squelching the hurt for the hundredth time, she turned and walked to the spare room.

And she ran back into the kitchen a minute later, panting, 'She's gone. Everything's gone!'

'What?'

'She's done a runner,' Anna said helplessly. 'She's left the baby, given her to me.'

CHAPTER THREE

'SHE's left the baby to me,' Anna repeated, hearing the dazed note in her voice—but it didn't sound as completely poleaxed as she felt right now. *She's left the baby to me...*

Jared stared, slowly blinked, frowned and then shook his head. 'No way. That only happens in movies and novels.'

'Well, it's happened to me now.' Not knowing what to think, still lost in the shock of it all, she thrust the letter she'd found lying on the spare bed at him. 'And it's happened to you, too.'

He opened the note, and, unable to believe it still, Anna followed each word from behind his shoulder.

I'm so sorry, Anna, Mr West. I can't do this anymore—I have to stop fooling myself. When you left to get Mr West, Anna, I knew it was my fault Mr West was in trouble. I knew I'd brought trouble on you both. Then

I looked at Melanie, and knew I'd only screw up her life, too. I want to finish university, become a doctor. Maybe I'm being selfish, but I'm only twenty. I'm not qualified for anything, and I don't even have a settled home. I can't give Melanie the life she deserves, and I want to be free to follow my dreams.

I'm going to get help for the depression, and if I still feel the same way when I'm better, I'm applying to return to university next semester. I'll contact you again in a month. Please don't call Child Services or the police, not yet. I'm asking you to take my little girl somewhere safe for a few weeks while I get help. I don't want my mother to get rid of her or give her to strangers. Melanie loves you already, Anna. Jarndirri would be a wonderful place for her to grow up. Will you take care of my little girl?

PS: I'll stay until I hear your car return, and know Melanie's safe. Tell her that her mummy really loves her.

Anna saw the wetness of tears fallen over the PS, and closed her eyes.

'It's unsigned,' was all he said after a long silence in which Anna could hear her heart beating, feel the blood pounding in her throat and wrists.

Lost in the emotion of the note, the soul-deep loss she could so readily identify with, Anna tilted her head. 'So?'

He didn't answer, but the frown between his brows was so deep it made a grooved V. 'We should call Tom Hereford, get his legal opinion, before we do anything.'

Fighting the rising of panic like water from a burst dam, she nodded. She took the phone from its cradle and thrust it at him. She couldn't speak coherently to Tom, Jarndirri's lawyer, if her life depended on it.

Jared punched in the number, got through to Tom in moments—an account like Jarndirri was too lucrative to lose—and told the lawyer every-thing, while Anna shifted from foot to foot and dug crescents in her palms with her nails.

'Okay, Tom, thanks for that. Yes, be in touch soon. Goodbye.' He turned to her, his eyes flat. 'In Tom's opinion, chances are that, with the mother's permission to take Melanie, we'd have the upper hand over anything Maggie claims, since she can't prove she's cared for the child in any way. But he said get to Jarndirri as quickly and quietly as we can. He said he'd never want to go up against Maggie Foster. Apparently she sued Rosie's father when he left, for all he was worth, and fought until the man was bankrupted. But in the eyes of the law, either with or without a signature, Rosie is Melanie's mother. Her wishes, in writing, will be seen as legal and binding, since she named us both. But our case is only strong as long as they believe we're together.'

Though she knew he was telling the truth, she felt her teeth grind together. Her nod felt curt, graceless, even though this was why she'd called him.

'They're not going to believe a pretty show, Anna. They'd have to have compelling evidence that we've reunited—and not just for the baby's sake. If Maggie finds out we have her and decides she wants her grandchild, she'd have a stronger claim than ours. And she'd go down fighting all the way.'

'I know,' she muttered.

'So what I'm asking you is—is this what you want? What you really want? Is this going to be worth the fighting—maybe years of fighting—to have her?'

Unable to hold back, she heard words tumbling from her mouth she'd give almost anything to keep to herself. 'This isn't about me—it's about a tiny baby and what she needs. But you know what I want—what I've always wanted. I want a baby—*my* baby—but you know I can never have that now. But I love Melanie.' What a pathetic understatement! Amid the pain of loss, oh, the joy and solace that beautiful baby's satin skin and drooling smile had given her in the past few months! That Rosie had *needed* her—that Melanie had needed her rather than Anna being the grieving, needing one—had been her saving grace, her road back to life when she'd begun losing it. 'I—I do want her,' she admitted quietly, giving up.

His gaze, when he lifted it to hers, held the cold distance he always showed when she'd displeased him. It left her shivering inside. 'This is the reason you wanted to see me, Anna? The only reason?'

She felt a flush creeping up her cheeks. 'When I called you, I thought it would only be for a few weeks,' she tried to snap, but her voice wobbled. 'I thought Rosie would worry about taking the baby flying so close to the Wet, but she wasn't. She said everyone knows you're the best small-plane pilot in the State.' The heat on her face suffused her throat as, if anything, his face turned to deep-freeze. 'I know you wanted me to come back—' *What am I doing, sounding like I want to go back to him?*

'This isn't about what I want,' he snarled. 'Tell me what *you* want, Anna.'

'Right now I don't *know* what I want. I don't know if this offer is real, or the depression talking. She's been in a bad way.' She wheeled around, began pacing the room. 'I want to help Rosie, to be there for Melanie—but this…' She sighed and shook her head. 'I can't believe she really means this. I doubt she's thought about what it will be like without Melanie. I don't want

Maggie involved, giving Melanie away before Rosie's made a firm decision. She needs a chance for the therapy to work before she decides on what she wants to do.' She gave him a look of intense pleading. 'She just needs a few weeks to get her life right, and…' Anna closed her eyes '…if she decides she wants to give Melanie away, I want to have a strong claim. I want to be a mother,' she whispered, feeling her throat close up and the rain fall from inside…

No. I will not cry. I won't! She swiped at eyes stinging with familiar pain. There was no point crying in front of Jared. He wouldn't let her *feel*, he never listened or let her *be*. He'd just find some solution, a way to fix it so she'd stop.

It took all her inner control to speak calmly, to say the words she'd rehearsed since reading the letter. 'Because Rosie named us both, I can't adopt her without you,' she said, forcing a sense of calm she was far from feeling.

Jared was the one pacing the room now, drumming his fingers hard on the kitchen counter as he passed it. 'This whole situation is insane, Anna. It hasn't got a snowball's chance in the equator of working.'

She felt her heart jerk. If she couldn't make Jared believe in this, he'd never go along with it and she'd lose her last chance at motherhood. 'It's not insane. It can work. Maggie won't know a thing about it.

She'll just assume Rosie left with Melanie. Rosie just needs a few weeks' peace,' she murmured, hearing the pleading note again. 'The authorities don't have to know for a few weeks, do they? Jarndirri's isolation is the perfect cover. We can send away all the hands—say I'm coming home, and we want a second honeymoon for a week or two. That way we can persuade them we were back together before Melanie came into our lives.'

'You've obviously been thinking fast. Go on, tell me the rest of your plan,' he said, his understatement a monument to self-control.

'There isn't much else.' For some reason she couldn't look at him as she stuttered, 'I—I love her, Jared. When I'm with her, my heart…well, it didn't heal, it never could after Adam, but…' *I almost forget when Melanie's here. I slept through the night for the first time since he died.* She raised her eyes to his, in a pleading that had been foreign to her proud, independent Curran nature until now. 'Please, Jared. We're not doing anything illegal. We're helping someone who desperately needs time out. We're just—just foster-parents for a few weeks, and then I'll go, leave Jarndirri to you for the rest of your life. Whether we reconcile for good or not is no one's business but ours.'

'It doesn't even seem like it's my business,' he replied, still with the sense of a well scraped dry: empty and not caring.

How did he *do* that? She couldn't bear the gaping hole inside her heart, and only Melanie had come close to filling it. Some days, all she wanted to do was fill it somehow, anyhow—and when people left their babies outside stores, left alone in a pram, the temptation almost killed her. *Don't leave your child, even for a moment! Don't you know how precious they are? Don't you understand some people would die to have your blessings?*

She couldn't believe Rosie would leave her child permanently.

But if Rosie meant it…

It would be the gift of her lifetime. Oh, for the chance to have chubby baby arms around her when she needed to feel loved—to hold a warm, *living* body close instead of the living death she'd endured the past year, always seeing her beautiful boy, cold in his tiny white coffin…

If helping Rosie—if having even a tiny chance of becoming this darling baby's mother—meant going back to Jarndirri for now, so be it.

When Jared half turned from her with that signature shrug of his—why should he care if she needed Melanie or not? He wanted his own kids, not this stranger baby—she panicked and blurted, 'If you do this, I'll sign all rights to Jarndirri over to you, permanently. Just let me stay until Rosie makes her decision—or until the adoption goes through. Let the authorities think we were together when Rosie asked us to take her. Let her stay with us through one Wet season so she'll be bonded to me by the time the adoption agency can get there. Then I'll leave with her, come back here or disappear, whatever you want.'

'Seems to me that *what I want* isn't in this scenario at all, apart from Jarndirri.'

The understated sarcasm sent a new flash of fear through her. She saw the frown on his half-averted face, and the harsh breaths jerking into his chest. Terrified she hadn't offered enough, she added anxiously, 'I swear if you do this, I'll give you whatever you want. I'll set you free…' she gulped hard and forced the words out '…to have the children you want with someone else. I'll give you Jarndirri, and all the money. I don't care. I don't want any of it. All I want is Melanie.'

He wasn't looking at her at all now. He'd wheeled right around, looking out the back window to the slow-brewing storm outside. 'Thank you.' Two words, cool irony.

The two words felt like an accusation. She flushed. 'I'm just trying to be honest. If you're honest with yourself, you know I'm right. You only wanted me because I was part of Dad's marry-her-for-Jarndirri package. Well, I'm giving you what you always wanted, free of strings.'

'That isn't what I signed on for when I married you.' He turned to the fridge, pulled out the milk.

'I think you were right that day in the hospital. If you think Jarndirri is all I want, you don't know me at all.' He lifted the sugar bowl. 'Still one sugar and milk, or has that changed about you, as well?'

'Still the same,' she sighed. Why did he have to make this so uncomfortable? She was what he'd always wanted her to be—sensible, unemotional, not putting her wants on him. Why was he changing the game on her now? 'Look, Jared, can't we deal with this as adults? You signed on for Dad's dream; you love the life on Jarndirri. You're willing to continue on there for the rest of your life. I'm the one walking away. You can have everything you wanted when you agreed to marry me…and I'll set you free. You can find another woman to have your sons with.'

There, she'd said it, twice now, and even without a quiver. So why wasn't he grateful? Surely she was letting him off lightly—but the silences were becoming unbearable. Jared looked outside as he poured coffee and stirred in the milk and sugar, his face expressionless, just as it had been the day her father had told them of his plans for them to marry and inherit Jarndirri together. She remembered the sick, sinking feeling, so scared he'd say yes, even more scared he'd say no…

Anna forced herself to stand still and quiet, giving him time and space to think.

Then he said the last thing she expected as he turned back to face her at last, pushing a mug toward her. 'Bryce offered me the Jarndirri deal with Lea, you know.'

She almost choked on her coffee. 'What?'

'When you were fifteen and Lea was eighteen, he said if I took Lea off his hands so he didn't have to worry about her any more, I could have everything.'

She frowned, forcing coffee down a tight throat. Thinking of it, it made perfect sense—Dad knew she'd be the good girl, accept his decision and take whatever was left. He had to get the rebel settled and safe before she did anything stupid to dishonour the Curran name. 'And?'

He shrugged. 'Predict it, Anna. You know Lea.'

She thought about it, and found herself grinning. 'She exploded, told Dad to go to hell… and you too, if you thought she was going to be served on anyone's platter.'

His brows lifted, fell. 'That's about it…you just missed one or two small things.'

'Well?' she prompted after a few moments.

His eyes met hers…deep, stormy grey-blue, his mouth curving in that half-smile of sensual intent, and she felt her body heating in response. She couldn't tear her gaze away; her breaths came short and choppy. He didn't move—he didn't have to. Whenever he looked at her like that, she always came to him…came running.

How easy I made everything for him. A loving wife and Jarndirri, all neatly served on Dad's platter. One kiss, one touch and I became his for the taking.

'And?' she croaked, forcing her feet to stay in place. Heart and mind fought a body that suddenly reminded her that, uterus or not, she was still a woman. Sort of.

'And we had a good laugh later. From the day I moved in, we were like brother and sister. There was nothing there.'

'Really?' She tried to snort the word, but it came out breathless. 'You two always got on so well.'

'Every way but one.' The smile slowly grew, and she felt her feet itching, trying to move. Her hands ached, screaming to touch him. She might not love him now, but, oh, he knew every way to arouse her, to give her satisfaction. 'She didn't want me either. We tried to kiss once, and ended up falling on the ground laughing.' He grinned now. 'She kept wiping her mouth and saying, "Ick, gross, it's like kissing my brother."'

'Did you like it?' she asked slowly, wishing she could keep the words locked inside, but so many years of wondering…

He took a step toward her, the predatory intent clear, and all the words she'd practised since asking him to come fled her mind. She watched him come, her body coming alive, hot and breath-less, her breasts swelling and her hands lifting…

'Kissing Lea was one of my life's happier memories. It was then I knew I had a sister for life—and I knew I'd never hurt her.'

Interpreting everything he hadn't said, as usual, she relaxed—until he took another step closer, body heat the oxygen fuelling her slow-burning body, and she gulped and breathed, trying to keep up with her galloping heart. 'And then?'

'I found you three weeks later in the haystack, hiding from Lea with the chocolate stash you stole,' he murmured, eyes languorous with blatant sexu-ality, and his tinder sparked the slow flame in her.

Hiding from Lea, she'd whispered frantically to Jared to not give her away when he found her there. He'd looked at her in silence, asking without words what on earth she was doing. She'd lifted the chocolate in laughing offer, sharing her booty if he wouldn't give her away. And he bent to her, saying she'd made a mess of her face, and took the chocolate smears from her mouth with his lips and tongue. She'd forgotten all about the chocolate, the hay in her hair and on her clothes; she wrapped her arms around his neck and kissed him back, crossing the unseen threshold from child to woman in an instant.

He hadn't kissed her again for a long time—she was only fifteen to his eighteen—but he hadn't gone with all the young guys to the infamous B&S balls—the Bachelor & Spinster balls—after that. And he hadn't let any other guy near her either. He'd kept her on constant sensual alert with burning-hot glances and unspoken promises, soft whispers in her ear and intimate jokes for her alone.

But on her eighteenth birthday he'd given her a beautiful diamond ring made especially for her with gold from Jarndirri and a Kimberley diamond, danced with her all night at her party, and took her outside to the high verandah where she kept dozens of sweet-scented potted flowers and her climbing roses—planting them, even in the high ground, would drown them in the Wet—and he'd kissed her again, this time deep and slow with his arms around her.

I'm going to marry you, he'd whispered in her ear after half an hour of dazzling, melting kisses, and, poor, starry-eyed girl that she'd been, she'd had no thought of denying him anything he'd wanted. They'd come back into the house with that ring on her left hand, and her eighteenth party had become their engagement party.

They'd married four years later, after she'd finished university as her father demanded. She'd come home, torn between wanting to teach and aching to be with the man she adored. One slow smile from Jared on her return to

Jarndirri, one melting kiss, and her future was decided. She couldn't have left him again if her life depended on it.

She'd never kissed any other man, had never wanted to. From the first time she'd seen him, she'd been lost; from the moment he'd kissed her in that haystack, his wishes had become her wishes, his world hers.

Then the bottom fell out of the world they'd forged for themselves, the shattering of dreams as beautiful as pure crystal, and just as delicate. When she came home from the hospital, she'd felt the storm building inside him slowly, worse for its being unspoken. He wanted her to talk, to come past her intense grief, to heal…but he only wanted her to say what he was ready to hear. She knew what he wanted—the smiles and laughter, the sensuality and return to the joyous woman she'd once been. He'd wanted relief from the endless pain, for the uncertainty to be over, so he could get on with his life.

He could get on with life, because *he* still had options. He could still become a father. He could never understand the depth of her double loss. He just wanted her sadness to be over so he could bring up what he'd planned. She felt the leashed impatience as the months passed.

That was Jared. He was willing to run any race, fight any fire, swim any flood…he'd be there whenever she needed him, for whatever reason she needed him, so long as she didn't expect him to talk, to share—or to *feel*. He just wanted to get on with it, whatever *it* was.

With Adam's death and the hysterectomy, she saw her life through new eyes: the compliance, the hollowness of trying to please a man who only saw her as his adjunct. What did she have that was all hers, that wasn't handed to her by her father, or given by Jared? What did she really want in life? It certainly wasn't the souvenir store.

She still didn't know what she wanted, and within an hour Jared's mere presence was threatening her determination to find it. He could shatter her newfound strength with the promise of a kiss—and, what was worse, she was almost giving in. With a kiss, he could make her want to come home for good—and she'd never know. Her life would again be Jared's to own.

She lifted her chin. 'While that's all sweet, it's really rather irrelevant now. I only want to come back until we hear from Rosie—and if she still wants us to adopt her, I'll give you Jarndirri, the money—whatever you want—if I can have Melanie.'

The long silence unnerved her—especially when he didn't move or step back. 'Is that a promise?' he asked slowly at last.

She frowned. 'What, about giving you…a

divorce?' She sipped her cooling coffee. Funny, after all the times she'd practised the word, it was still so hard to say. 'Of course, I told you—'

'That isn't what you said,' he interrupted her, his voice uncompromising. 'You promised me everything I want, if I let you stay.'

He wants more than Jarndirri...

Her stomach hollowed out. What little coffee she'd drunk churned inside, making her want to be sick. Twelve years together, five years married, so much they'd been through together, and still what she wanted meant nothing to him. A million hectares of earth still held his heart captive—that, and the life he'd planned for them. That was Jared, stubborn to the last.

I can't give you children, she wanted to scream. *I can't go back to where my sweet Adam was still here, still alive!*

Jarndirri was no longer home to her; it was the place where hope and dreams and love and laughter had died. All she wanted was to never go back.

For Melanie, her heart whispered. *You'll have Melanie.*

She forced her chin up. Her fists curled, she drew in a breath and said with a semblance of calm, 'Everything you wanted that I can give you, Jared.'

'Everything I wanted, Anna,' he repeated, his voice hard and cold. 'A little white lie or a big black one, I'll still be committing perjury for you. Give me your word.'

'I can't give you the babies you wanted,' she snapped, trying to hold in the tears. 'How can you even think I could—?'

Not a muscle in his face moved. He looked like the red rocks of the Kimberleys: wind-blasted, refusing to falter or weather away under pressure—and, illogically, she felt the stirring of arousal return. Was she a masochist, yearning for a man who didn't know how to feel? 'Just give me the promise, Anna. Then I'll do whatever it takes to give you that baby.'

Something turned to lead within her. She knew what he was demanding—her, back in his bed; back in his life and world. The Curran–West dynasty intact, with no more embarrassing separations…and she knew, looking in his eyes, he had another brilliant plan for them to have a baby. His baby, at least.

She ought to have known he wouldn't let her bail on him, or the life he loved. The opinion of their neighbours—his reputation, and keeping his promise to Bryce Curran, the only person he'd ever looked up to—meant that much to him.

He didn't want Melanie—but she couldn't see what he *did* want, or what he was planning. She only knew when he had an ace up his sleeve, and he always knew when to play it. This was only step one. He wanted his wife to come home with him—to share his bed again—and wasn't above using Melanie to get what he wanted.

All or nothing: that was Jared. Win at any cost.

She closed her eyes, shutting him out as her mind raced. She'd survived five years of marriage with plenty of desire and Jarndirri to bond them, but no love—at least on his side. She was a Curran, a strong Outback woman. And love it or hate it, Jarndirri was still home. She could never deny that. Love and hate and grief, it held her captive as strongly as it did Jared.

'You have my word.' She looked at him, and to her surprise felt only sadness as she said, 'But you need to know the truth. I'm only doing it for Rosie, and for Melanie. I would never have called you but for this dilemma. I'd never go back to you willingly, if I didn't have to. I want a life of my own. I was waiting until the year was up to divorce you.'

'And you've made me thoroughly aware of that fact for the past five months,' he said, his voice rich with irony, yet somehow as dry as dust.

Hearing some unaccustomed feeling beneath the coldness he was projecting, she wished it was different, that she could be happy about returning. 'I'm sorry, Jared. That's the way it is.'

At least, it was the way it had to be. She had a few weeks to convince the authorities they were a united couple—if spending those weeks in

Jared's bed could give her Melanie, a life and a future without the unbearable agony of the past year, she'd do it. Then, when she had the stamped, legal adoption papers in her hands, she'd prove to Jared it really was over. She'd make him believe she didn't care about anything but Melanie. If she could prove to him that he no longer had the power to move or hurt her, she'd walk away with her baby, and he'd be free to find a woman who could give him what she no longer could.

He'd thank her for it one day.

'Then come home,' he said, with no emotion at all now, not even triumph. 'I assume you have everything packed?'

And even though she deserved it, something inside her churned at his uncaring tone. She'd turned him off at last; she should be rejoicing. He was on his way to accepting it was over—if she could hold it together, stay strong, he'd let her go when the adoption went through, let her go find a life with Melanie, and he'd…

She shuddered at the thought of the man who'd always been hers belonging to anyone else— *having the children he'd craved from her, and she'd yearned to give.*

This was a sacrifice she had to be prepared to make. Part of her would always care about Jared, would always ache and burn when he moved on and had those children, but she couldn't live the life he loved any more. Why shouldn't he find happiness with a woman who wanted the life she'd abandoned?

'Yes, I have everything packed, and given notice to my landlord.' She kept her tone cool, reserved. 'I've closed the store until further notice.'

'Good. So drink the coffee. I assume we wait until the baby's awake.'

'Her name's Melanie,' she amended through clenched jaws.

He shrugged and reached for his coffee, downing it in a gulp. He never minded drinking it however he found it, hot or cold. 'I'm heading out. I have my phone. Call me when she wakes.'

He was out the door before she could speak. A chill raced down her neck, leaving her shivering with cold in the oppressive Kimberley heat. He was withdrawing from her at last, giving up—and though she ought to be celebrating, although she should think ahead to her life with Melanie, all she felt was a curious regret, an unfathomable emptiness.

Jared made it as far as the other end of the path leading to the beach from her place, safe from her sight, before his legs couldn't go farther. He heaved in breaths that seemed to take no air in because he kept wheezing. He held onto one of the thick trunks used for fencing posts along the track, bent almost double over it, dizzy and sick. He'd made it to the end of their deal without showing her what she'd done to him. He wouldn't be weak, like his father had been with his mother, using love to make her stay, pleading for her to fix the un-fixable…

I'd never go back to you willingly.

He kept his eyes squeezed tight shut. He hadn't realised how much hearing the words would hurt, because Anna wouldn't lie to him. If she said it, she meant it.

'No. It's grief speaking. She doesn't know what she wants,' he gasped through gritted teeth, between gasping breaths. 'It's not over. She'll come back to me. She'll love Jarndirri again once she's there. Everything will be like it used to be. I just—need—to stick to the plan.'

That was it: he needed to focus on the final result. This was no different from his other long-term plans. He'd had no results from planting the saltbush until two seasons had passed. He'd planted crops every year, not knowing if they'd be harvested or fail. He'd plant seeds with Anna now, give her everything she wanted, and wait to reap the benefits.

But what *did* she want? He knew squat about women's emotional needs, but some gut-deep instinct told him he hadn't reached the heart of her need to run from Jarndirri. Or why she'd needed to run from him.

Their loss should have brought them closer. Why hadn't it? Why had she never shared her loss with him, and allowed him to comfort her? Adam had been his son, too.

Adam...

He set his jaw so hard his teeth hurt, but it stopped the stinging of his eyes. He wasn't weak like his dad. He'd be strong for her, no matter what.

He hadn't won her back to him with all he'd tried. The past two weeks it felt as if he'd run slam into the boulder of limitations he'd never known he had—the eternal lack of understanding that stood between man and woman.

I can't stand being alone any more, she'd said in her note. Something about that sentence haunted him. He couldn't get everything she'd said—or was it what she *hadn't* said—out of his mind. Unable to understand, unable to forget them, all he had to do was find a way to bring her home. By now he was desperate enough to seduce, kidnap, bargain—whatever it took. Everything would be fine once they were home.

She wants a baby...and now she's got one, his mind whispered, *but only if I help her. She needs me now.*

Maybe all she needed was an excuse to come home?

Step one achieved, thanks to a dumped baby. Was that tiny scrap of humanity the small miracle he needed to get his life, his wife back?

CHAPTER FOUR

'THAT'S what I said, Ollie. Take a week off—everyone. Go away somewhere on full pay. Anna's coming home with me, and we want the place to ourselves,' Jared said to the station's foreman over the chopper's radio, sounding clipped, just a touch embarrassed. Outback men did *not* do emotion, and especially not in front of other men.

'How're we gonna get out of here now, Jared?' The surprise was clear in Ollie's voice, but the curiosity was under tight control. This was *personal* stuff, and the one thing the Jarndirri men did well, besides work from before dawn to after dusk, was keep their own stuff locked under a tight drum. Following the example set them for years by her father: real men did not share their feelings; they worked, played football and drank beer. Bonding, talking was what women did. 'The Wet's about an hour from starting—'

'Take the other plane—the Jeeps are too dangerous with the Wet coming. Stay at a town or resort, take the wives and girlfriends—it's on me.' He spoke in a light tone, but he kept throwing glances back at a sleeping Melanie.

Anna was similarly anxious. If she woke up and Ollie heard the wails…

'John and Ellie Button won't want to go anywhere,' Ollie argued, while Anna became more and more nervous. 'Jarndirri's their only home unless they visit their kids, which they don't do in the Wet.'

'Then make it clear they're on paid leave. I can't leave Jarndirri, but we want time on our own.' He was back to that stiff awkwardness that told Ollie to *back off*.

'You'll need help, even in the Wet—'

'Anna will help me. She knows the place backwards, and it's only for a week. Will you stop arguing, Ollie, and take the holiday?'

Filled with urgency, Anna leaned to his ear. 'Don't say any more to him, or it will look suspicious,' she whispered, feeling the heat of him warm her shivers, relieving her fears just by being here. Jared was so good at thinking on his feet, and finding the solution to any emergency—as perfect at it as he was at flying. Though the winds were fickle and lightning flickered in the distance, the Cessna hadn't so much as wobbled. He was in full control, plane and life.

He nodded at her warning. 'We'll be there in a few hours. Feed the animals and corral them first.' He signed off without saying anything as sappy and uncharacteristic as *Have a good holiday.* Like the harsh red land they flew over, massive monolithic rocks that looked like God's marbles, the deep, inaccessible rivers and impossible waterfalls spread across Jarndirri, the men were silent, rugged, remote—and strangely unforgettable. Haunting her soul: they were *her* men, her land. She could leave, she could run, start a new life anywhere, but a part of her heart would always be here in the Kimberleys.

Turning, she looked at the sleeping form in the car seat—Melanie had a dreaming smile on her face— and Anna felt that gaping, shell-blasted hole inside her soul touched again with balm, sweet as baby powder, absolute as the trust this baby girl gave her.

It would never heal. She could never forget Adam, would never stop aching for the other babies that never had the chance to live because of her thin uterus walls. But when this beautiful baby was with her, she felt *alive* again. Even if it was for a few weeks, a few months, she'd take the time with Melanie…and then, maybe, she'd find the strength to walk away from the only real home she'd ever known, to divorce the only man she'd ever loved and still wanted, even if she wasn't in love with him now—

'Don't think about it.'

She started and pulled herself together. 'What?'

His gaze met hers, his strong, calm. 'You'll be a mother—either of this baby, or another. Don't give up hope. It's going to happen.'

His eyes held the depth of a thousand words unspoken. Anna felt a juddering shiver touch her neck. Again he'd known her heart was bleeding, and he was always there…

There finding a solution for her, because he had to make everything right and he didn't do emotion—and she'd held onto his solutions like a lifeline for too many years. *We can do IVF, Anna. We can try again, Anna. Just one more try for a baby, Anna. I know it's been tough on you, but think of the end result—the baby you've craved for years.*

That was what he'd always say: *It's been tough on you, the baby you want,* as if losing four babies hadn't affected him at all.

Had any of it hurt him, made him feel the loss as acutely as she had? Until Adam, she hadn't truly known. He'd never shown any emotion during those years. He'd kept on working, planning for the next child. But when Adam had died, he'd cried in her arms; and the echoes of his cry when she'd collapsed the next day still rang in her heart.

Anna! For God's sake, someone, help us!

But the feeling, the emotional connection she'd yearned to know in the man she'd loved all her life seemed to be no more than a day's aberration. The old unemotional Jared had returned the moment he'd been back on Jarndirri soil a week later, working from four in the morning till six at night as usual. The only hint of emotion he'd showed had been a state of repressed anger and the sense of exhausted patience at her ongoing grief and refusal to touch him, or share their bed.

Even today, when she was close to the sharing he claimed he wanted to hear, it was no different. *Don't get depressed, Anna, you'll be a mother.*

He'd been dry-eyed at his father's funeral, at her father's funeral. Even after the hysterectomy, he'd been calm, focussed on her pain, her loss. *We'll find a way, Anna.* But he'd cried when Adam had died. For a whole hour, he'd cried…

'Thank you.' Stilted words through a tight throat; she didn't know what else to say. Like her dad, Jared held to the old code of honour: *Never back down, never surrender. Always keep your word.* He'd married her, so he'd stick to her for life. She knew he'd do his best to never show her the resentment, how cheated he was that she'd never given him a son.

Regret was weakness to Jared; divorce would be seen as the ultimate failure.

She'd already been through a failure, a loss and

madness so deep and profound that divorce could only be dessert after a heavy main course—it would almost feel like sweet relief.

Almost.

'She'll have to make do with a bed pushed against the wall with chairs for a day or two, until I can fly to Geraldton to get some baby things,' he said, his voice flat.

She frowned at him. 'Why? Where are…the things we had for Adam…?' She almost choked, saying it. Her arms and heart ached with useless longing.

In the ten seconds that followed their son's name she heard every beat of her heart.

'I gave them away.' His voice was taut.

Her heart jerked, and one shoulder moved forward, not a shrug but a tiny movement that showed too much. 'When?'

'Three weeks ago.' Jared had turned back to the horizon, watching where he flew. The flight path was one he knew like his own skin, but he wasn't looking at her. Jared could always look her in the face as he talked about *her* emotions, but she doubted he even acknowledged his own existed. 'The Lowes needed some new things for their baby.'

That was it, all he had to say about destroying their son's nursery? The last vestiges of their son's life had been pulled apart…the Lowes had eight kids now, by her count. It was so unfair. They had the kids *and* the things she'd made or painted for Adam with her own hands.

She nearly choked on the fury, the gut-level jealousy she'd never lose. 'And you never thought to ask me about it?'

Her pulse beat so hard against her throat, she heard it beating. Ten, nine, eight, seven, six… *boom-boom, boom-boom*… 'You hung up on me.'

She turned to look out the window. They were flying over the mining community of Tom Price. The scattered houses and gaping holes in the earth looked so lonely from up here. 'I see.'

After a long silence, he said in a quiet voice that hid all emotion, 'Say it, Anna.'

She shrugged, as if she didn't care. 'What's the point? It's done.'

He said nothing in response, and she refused to make it easy for him. She kept looking at the world below while everything they weren't saying grew legs and arms, put a timer device together on the bomb of silence and set it ticking down. The unseen contest had no winners because he never spoke, and she had nothing to say—or too much. Fury, jealousy, betrayal and all the useless regret…

She had to stop this, find accord with Jared somehow, or they'd never survive the next few weeks together. Why didn't Melanie wake up? If she'd make a single sound...

Three, two, one—

'They're in danger of losing everything.'

It took her a moment to realise what he meant. He'd taken the safe option, talking of the nursery furniture and the Lowes. She should have known he would. Jared had never had to reach out to her—he waited for her to come to him, to tell him what she needed, so he could fix it. She had always gone to him—until she'd had nothing left to say, nothing left to ask him to fix.

Countdown reset, defences built, places of refuge established. Husband and wife stared out of separate windows, facing each other down from either side of a silent battleground. It was Christmas detente, meeting in the middle for a meaningless game of football, knowing hostilities would soon be resumed. Too much had been left unsaid between them, too many emotions buried in the trenches of memory. The fragile cobweb of deception for the sake of a baby was the only thing holding them together.

'Fair enough,' was all she said in response, trying to dull the sharp edge of the bayonet she'd been stabbing him with. What was the point? His armour was impenetrable.

Three, two, one—

'I thought you'd understand. People matter

more than things. Isn't that what you always said every time you gave our things away to someone in need?' he growled out of nowhere.

'I'm surprised you remember that,' she replied without inflection.

'I remember everything.' His gaze was cold, and again she shivered. When she didn't answer, he sighed with the exaggerated patience she hated. 'Tell me what's going on in your head, Anna. We've got to find a way to put this right, climb out of this crazy mess we're in.'

At least he was finally asking, instead of telling her to come home, or using his body to bring her to capitulation; but didn't he know that, if he had to ask what she wanted, it was useless to her? 'There's nothing either of us can do, Jared. There's no solution. Nothing can change what's done. It's over.'

'Obviously—that's why you called me, why you're here now.'

The frozen tone put her on the defensive. 'I don't know any other man who keeps secrets the way you do, who hides emotion so well. If you *have* any emotion.'

He made some adjustments to their flight path. He frowned hard at the horizon, as if there was imminent danger. 'One day you're going to have to face that what happened last year happened to us both, instead of thinking it was only your pain, your sorrow. One day you'll know running from it does nothing.'

'I didn't *run* from anything. I *left* you.' She felt her nostrils flare as she dragged in air. 'Just because we aren't together any more doesn't mean I haven't faced it—all of it.' *What I lost—and what I am.* Cold and shivering to her soul, she'd faced it. She had no choice: Adam came to visit her nightly, that cold, sweet, sleeping face. Eternal sleep in a cold white casket instead of the sky-blue cradle they'd made for him, with stencils of Donald Duck and Mickey Mouse…the pretty mobiles dangling above for him to laugh at, to reach for…

'You never talked about it.'

Anna heard a disbelieving laugh, a half-sneer in it, and part of her didn't believe it had come from her; she'd never heard it come from her lips before. Yet she was glad for the distraction. 'So which are you in this scenario, the pot or the kettle?'

Very quiet, so quiet she barely heard him over the plane's rumble, he said, 'The doctors told me to wait for you to start.'

'And of course that was the only thing stopping you,' she retorted. 'You're just a pillar of communication. Always so open with what you feel.'

He didn't answer that—and in the silence something in her snapped. 'That's it, Jared, retreat into your own head, don't tell me anything. I always made it so easy for you, didn't I? I did the talking, the loving, and you didn't have to try. That's what's getting to you, isn't it? For the first time in twelve years I'm not blurting out my every feeling and emotion to you, so you can work out how to fix it all. I walked out, and didn't want or need your solutions or to make things right—and you couldn't handle it. For months you've been the one coming to me, but I didn't come home as you expected. How embarrassing has it been for you? The Great Jared West is a failure with his own wife. Is everyone laughing at you—or, worse, pitying you?'

She waited, her heart pounding hard. After long moments, he spoke without emotion. 'It's nothing I'm not used to. And I'm still here.'

Anna blinked, blinked again. What did that *mean*? The cold, emotionless Jared West, the King of Jarndirri, had actually felt like a failure at some point in his life?

A little wail came from behind as she tried to work out what he was trying to tell her. As ever, his verbal economy hid a wealth of secrets, but she didn't have the tools to dig for it.

The baby's wail grew in decibels. She sounded frightened.

Relieved to have something to do, she unbuckled her seat belt and moved to Melanie. She picked her up and cuddled her, crooning to the baby, but Melanie's cries grew stronger. As Anna sat in a back seat, Melanie began head-butting Anna, screaming now, pulling at her ears and staring at Anna in pleading and indignation combined.

Helpless, she said out loud, 'What's wrong with her? She seems really upset. Maybe she's hungry, or her nappy needs changing?'

She didn't really expect an answer—so she started when Jared said, 'The unfamiliar surroundings probably confused her, and cabin pressure in planes often upsets babies. They don't know how to pop their ears, so the pressure grows until it hurts. Give her a bottle, or a pacifier. The sucking motion will pop her ears, and stop the pain.'

He was right. The moment Anna unwrapped the warmed bottle from the foil—a makeshift warmer—and put the teat in Melanie's mouth, the baby sucked frantically, and the mottled colour in her face faded. She left off pulling her ears, and grabbed at the bottle, sucking hungrily. Then she smiled at Anna around the teat, making a milky mess of her face, and Anna's heart nearly exploded with joy and love. Beautiful, darling girl…

'Give her a teething rusk when she's finished with the bottle. Chewing or sucking relieves the pressure on her ears,' Jared called back a minute later.

Anna didn't even want to question his authority—a course of wisdom proven right when Melanie grabbed at the hard-baked bread called a teething rusk with a gurgle of happiness.

'Thank you,' she said much later, as the baby sat back in the adapted car seat, nappy changed, making a gruel-mess all over her face with the rusk. 'How did you know?'

'Dad taught me to fly when I was twelve,' he said briefly.

'And?' she pushed, when he didn't embellish. Jared so rarely spoke of his father, who'd died when he'd been fourteen.

'Nicky was about that age. Mum asked me to take him up with Dad and Andie one day when he was teething, and she needed an hour's sleep. She loaded us up with bottles and teething rusks for the cabin pressure—but though she packed one, she forgot to tell us to change his nappy.' Jared chuckled. 'She gave us all a serve about his nappy rash that night.'

Taken aback by the unexpected intimacy of the memory shared, Anna couldn't help wondering why he'd told her—he'd never once shared anything meaningful or joyful about his childhood with her. 'So who grovelled to her the most?' she teased, keeping it light, hiding her intense curiosity. She knew so little of him outside the work yards and bedroom.

'Dad.' That was it, no embellishment. She ought to have known he wouldn't say more—and yet the single word held cadences in all shades of the rainbow: resignation, bitterness, anger and a world of pain unhealed. The numbness of endless loss—

Maybe he'd understand how she felt more than she'd assumed?

She'd heard the rumours that his father had killed himself when he'd lost the West property, Mundabah Flats…but Jared had never said a word about it to her, either in denial or confirmation. As if it hadn't happened…or it hadn't affected him in the least. He'd just come to Jarndirri, found a new father, a new property to run, and he'd gone on with life as if nothing had changed.

No. They stood looking at the same rainbow, but from opposite ends. He kept digging for the pot of gold when she'd long ago decided there was nothing left to find.

'How's your mother?' Such a mundane question, but she had to start somewhere. And when she saw his face shut down before he spoke, it felt as if she'd used a key to a door she hadn't known existed.

'Fine. She's getting married.'

'Oh,' she said, feeling blank. Though she was a very attractive woman, Pauline West hadn't even seen a man since Jared's father's death sixteen years ago. 'When?'

'Six weeks.' Jared's voice was flat. 'His name's Michael Anglesey. He's another failed farmer—she must have a thing for them. They want to marry at Mundabah Flats, and take up running the place again. She wants me to give her away—and she's asked for enough money to start the place going again.'

'Well, what's the problem? We can afford it,' she replied without thinking. Reverting to thinking of them as Jared and Anna, King and Queen of Jarndirri, was just so easy.

In the tic at his jaw she saw another multi-hued silence, resonating like glass about to shatter. Resisting the urge to touch his hand—so much tension in him, he'd never returned to the West property of Mundabah since his father had died, even though he'd poured money hand over fist to make the property thrive—she stuck to the simple questions. 'How do you feel about her marrying, and them running Mundabah?'

'I don't want the place. Someone might as well run it.' He shrugged. 'We land soon.' Shutting the door on her again, as always.

'Fine,' she said tightly. 'I'll go sit in the back with Melanie.'

Jared made a harsh sound as she unbuckled her seat belt again, needing distance. 'What do you want me to say, Anna?'

'Nothing.' She forced blandness into her tone,

as if she wasn't burning with the betrayal of his unconscious rejection. 'I don't want anything from you but a few lies.' *Nothing you've ever been willing to give.* 'We pretend we're back together until Melanie's either back with Rosie or the adoption has gone through, and then I'm gone.'

'That's not the deal.'

She sighed, standing between the two front seats. 'You're not going to say it, are you? You want me to say it for you, make life easy, just as I always have?'

'I want you to talk, Anna,' he said quietly. A double-edged sword in six words. Saying everything and nothing at all.

'Yeah, well, we all want someone to talk to us,' she mocked, 'and some of us had it, and some of us got nothing.' Silence greeted her taunt, and she snapped. 'Fine, I'll talk, but I doubt you'll want to hear it. You want me back in your bed until I leave. You want me to pretend for the sake of the workers and our neighbours I'm back for good, that I'm madly in love with you, and we're going to make a family with Melanie. Okay, whatever.' She snorted out a laugh, and shrugged. 'I can put on a show—I might even enjoy the sex, it always was a good stress relief when you drove me crazy with your silence—but that's all it will be. If you're expecting to make me love you again, forget it. It's dead, Jared—*dead.*'

She forced her gaze to stay on him, her chin up. Did her hammering heart show the truth: the lady doth protest too much? She might not love him any more—only heaven knew how she felt about anything but Melanie right now—but on a purely physical level she still wanted him, ached for his touch. She hadn't wanted it at all after the hysterectomy—it felt too much like a farce, trying to pretend she was a normal woman still. But some time in the past five months since she'd left him, her body had awoken again.

Probably with that first kiss he'd planted on her when he'd come to Broome.

As if he'd heard her thoughts, he said coolly, 'You keep telling yourself that—but you kissed me back yesterday. And the time before that, and the time before that.'

A sigh came out from between clenched teeth. 'It's been over a year since I slept with anyone, and you're the only man I've been with—you made sure of that. What else do I know but you? What else can I compare you to? I'm *the* Mrs West. I've been untouchable in the eyes of almost everyone in the Kimberleys from the time I was fifteen.'

Slowly, as if he'd thought about her words before they'd come, he said, 'And I've been *the* Mr Curran since I was eighteen.'

She sighed. 'As usual, you've taken my point

and changed its direction to suit you. Tell me, did you always equate sex with love, Jared? Did you ever know me at all? In all the years you took my love for granted, from fifteen to now, did you ever ask yourself if I was happy, or if the life you wanted and planned for us both was what I wanted out of life?'

'Sit down and strap in, Anna, we're approaching the runway,' was his only answer, as he began pushing the wheel forward, leading by the nose.

The plane lost altitude, making her sit abruptly. She looked out over the wide red land with its patches of cultivated grass for the animals, brown and dry from early summer, not yet green with the drenching of the Wet. The house, creamy yellow with the rust-red tin roof, sat like a proud island of beauty in the wild, arid surrounds. It sat there in pride and defiance against the odds and the elements.

Jarndirri: home and yet not, a place where happiness had always seemed to elude her. Always trying to be perfect, and always failing. How could she have lived here almost all her life, miss it so much when she wasn't here, and yet always return with such a feeling of conflicted fatalism? Had the stones judged her unworthy of a normal life here?

'Look, Anna. Look at the beauty, the perfection,' Jared said as she clipped herself in. He swept his hand around the intense, wild beauty. 'How could you not be happy here? What else did you—what more could you want from life than what we have?'

Intense loneliness filled her at the incredulity in his question. That was it, the conflict that lay between them. Jarndirri was everything to him; how could she want more, apart from raising a family? To him there *was* nothing more. Jared loved Jarndirri, would have loved Adam, had he lived. But he'd never loved her. She was The Curran, the means to the life he wanted…especially once she'd responded to his kiss, after Lea hadn't.

'What I wanted then is immaterial,' she said over the roar of the landing plane, refusing to indulge in self-pity. 'What I want now also seems immaterial.'

He waited until he'd slowed the engine speed to a crawl before he spoke. 'It's immaterial to me, you mean?'

She shrugged. 'It doesn't matter. If I have Melanie, I can put up with the rest.'

The plane moved gently into the open hangar. 'Would you like to spell out what "the rest" is?' he asked, in a tone bordering on dangerous: his *don't go there* voice. But he was asking—and she felt reckless. Too many years wasted, playing the Golden Girl, first for Dad and then for Jared. Being what everyone wanted, until she no longer knew who she was.

Now she didn't have to. She'd lost everything she'd ever wanted.

It was time to take back, to have a life that belonged to *her*, not hemmed in and surrounded by the expectations or happiness of others.

'Life in a house with people who expect me to be The Curran, just like my father. Life on a property so isolated the loneliness became my only friend, the only one I could talk to.' She turned away from the look in his eyes, as hard as coal crystallising into a diamond, and just as black. 'Being tied to a man who wants things I can never give, and has never given me the one thing I truly want.'

'There's one thing you want, asleep behind us,' he replied in a voice so cold she shuddered beneath the ice he poured on her. 'If Rosie doesn't come back, I'll be committing perjury to give you what you want, despite the sugar coating you put on it. Little white lies are worth prison time if anyone finds out.'

'Yes,' she managed to say, feeling small and almost sick at his ruthless ripping apart of her delusions. 'But while I'm truly grateful, I don't want to sleep with you again.'

'I don't remember saying I expected that—or that I wanted it.'

At his cool, amused tone, a heat far drier than the steam-room kind seeping into the plane now the engine was off scorched her cheeks. 'You kissed me like that. I guess I assumed it's what you wanted.'

He lifted one shoulder: his *I couldn't care less* shrug. 'I thought you wanted to come back. Jarndirri's half yours—and you're the real Curran. Kissing used to make you happy.'

Swallowing the unexpected lump in her throat, she closed her eyes and willed control. Why did she ever bandy words with him, or expect to get her point across? His few words could always slay her into silence. 'All right, Jared. You win,' she said wearily. 'You always do.'

Jared swore with efficient fluency, rough and angry. 'Anna, that isn't what I wanted.'

Too numb to get into an argument she knew she'd only lose, she muttered, 'Then why won't you look me in the eye when you say it?'

Silence met her reluctant challenge.

She shrugged. 'It doesn't matter. You always end up getting everything you want, one way or another. I don't think you could stand to lose at anything.' When he turned to look at her then, moving closer as if to touch her, hold her—knowing it always softened her—she shook her head. 'Can you please see if it's clear to go into the house?' she whispered, fighting tears with everything she had. She'd shed enough for a lifetime.

After a moment that hung between them like a corpse, he swore again and climbed out of the cockpit, stalking to the house across the half-acre of yard that had once been her little veggie patch in dry season.

To her surprise, Jared walked in the straight lines of the plough, because her little patch of ground wasn't dead. There were green shoots of carrots, the lumps for potatoes and onion, and full heads of broccoli and cabbage everywhere.

She was surprised someone had cared enough to plant more. It was probably Mrs Button, who appreciated that they didn't have to fly in vegetables every week.

Lifting Melanie out of the car seat, she cuddled the baby and waited in the shadows of the hangar until Jared returned. She wasn't in a hurry to go back to the house: the beautiful pale yellow homestead with double-glazed windows and wide verandahs that had been her mother's and grandmother's and great-grandmother's home before her, but had never felt like hers.

So many Currans had lived at Jarndirri, with so much history—so much of it forever unspoken. Strong women had married tough, silent men who had worked the land, struggled against the elements and illness, women who'd borne their children in the rooms inside that house because doctors hadn't existed out here. The Curran women were the perfect complements for their men. Even her mother had taken six long years to surrender to the breast cancer that had killed her, and had only taken to her bed after four of those years. Until then she'd worked the land, run the house, looked after their staff and cared for her daughters, even given birth to her, Anna—she'd been given the breast cancer diagnosis when she'd been pregnant.

And she, the last Curran woman, had only ever felt like a fake. Less than a woman, less than strong, bonded to the land in a love-hate relationship because it had taken the only thing she'd ever wanted from her. She'd even risked her life to try one final time for a child when the doctors had advised against it, because Jared needed a son.

'They've all gone.'

Jared's voice soaked into her consciousness like the history of this, the land she loved and loathed—and she wondered when he'd become a part of that love and loss and hate. She nodded. 'Go and do what you have to. I'll get the bags once Melanie's settled.' Words as dead and emotionless as her heart felt.

As she walked past him, holding Melanie against her like a shield and bulwark against the enemy, he said, low and fierce, 'I didn't want to win, Anna.'

For a moment she almost turned back. He touched her shoulder, and she shuddered with her body's betrayal of her heart. 'Then why does talking to you, touching you, always feel like a contest I've already lost?'

When he didn't answer, she moved out of the hangar into the bright-and-darkness of the heavy-clouded air, thick like soaked cotton wool, glistening with diamond-bright moisture and a touch of sunlight breaking through in tiny slivers.

Coming home again felt like a farewell. The beginning of the end…and this time goodbye would be for ever. She couldn't go through this again—and after Melanie's life was settled, one way or the other, she hoped to have the strength to leave Jared and Jarndirri for ever, and, finally, never yearn to come back.

CHAPTER FIVE

JARED took his time feeding the animals in the massive sheds on the high ground, and making sure the gates were securely closed and the electric alarms on—the storm was closing in hard now—before returning to the homestead. He kept trying to think of what to do to get things back to the way they used to be with Anna; but even after all the years of being her lover and husband, and after everything they'd been through together, he felt as if he was locked inexorably in square one.

Her words kept chiming in his head like a bell tolling. *Talking with you always feels like a contest I've already lost.* Well, he knew how it felt now. That was how he'd felt every time she'd thrown him out of her place at Broome. And if he hated it, if he couldn't stand being in last place with her, how had always losing made her feel? In his driving need to do it all, be it all, to win at any cost, had he left her behind, left her out in the cold and, worse, not even noticed?

Maybe it's time things changed. Maybe it's time we both won.

He strode in through the back verandah to the kitchen. After a spare breakfast and no lunch, he was more than ready for dinner—but there was nothing cooking. Anna was no cook, but she could do a steak and salad when Mrs Button was sick, so why hadn't she…?

Distant cries gave him his answer. He followed the wailing sound to the spare room where she'd slept for so many months. Anna's bags were on the floor, unopened, but the baby's things were strewn all over.

So she was still resisting coming back to their room? He squashed the urge to grab her bags and take them where they belonged—for now. He'd change her mind soon enough. He'd make her melt for him…

Then he forgot his needs, his plans. Holding the baby, jiggling her in an awkward attempt at comfort, Anna was striding the floor, totally frazzled as the baby wailed without let-up.

He knew better than to offer help with the baby right now. 'Should I make our dinner, or warm a bottle for her?' He took care to not sound superior or triumphant. *This isn't a contest between us, Anna—and whatever it is, I haven't won in a long time.*

'She's had a bottle, had her nappy changed.

She doesn't have a fever or anything. I've tried playing with her, singing to her—I don't know what to do,' Anna all but wailed.

He frowned, looking at the baby. She seemed more angry than exhausted, and she'd slept really well on the plane. A thought occurred to him. 'How old do you think she is?'

Anna wheeled around on him, flushed and pretty in her dishevelment, and needing him…at least for now. And she was holding a baby in her arms…but it wasn't his baby son, his Adam.

Jared ached, thinking of what could have been—if the baby was Adam he'd have the right to hold him, to kiss her better, to walk him at night—anything to lighten Anna's load. He'd look into his son's eyes and feel that love, that bond— the sense of future, of destiny fulfilled.

Adam…

'Rosie started coming around three months ago, and she was…' She frowned down in anxiety at the baby, whose face was mottled and her wails upgrading to ear-piercing shrieks. 'She must be about six months—why?'

'At that age, babies eat stuff like mashed bananas and vegetables,' he said gruffly, still locked into the pain of useless longing for his son, his child, and for the loving wife he'd somehow lost. *You always end up getting what you want.* 'Cereals too. Mum gave us all cereal.'

'I fed her this morning,' she replied in clear impatience. 'There was cereal in her bag.'

'Mum always fed the babies at night, too—usually vegetables or cereal with banana or mashed apple in it. She said they slept better. If the baby's used to that, not eating would make her cranky.'

'But she threw out the teething rusk I gave her and screamed louder,' she retorted, looking like she was about to tear her hair—or already had, by the looks of her. Apart from the lack of chocolate smears, she looked as she had the day he'd first kissed her, all mussed and kissable…

But lustful thoughts weren't going to help either of them now. She was trying to get this right on her own and failing—and he had minutes to help her before she turned away from him.

So he grinned at her to lighten her lack of knowledge. 'Have you ever tasted those things?'

She caught the smile, and her eyes glimmered in return, her mouth slowly curving. 'Obviously not for too long a time. So it's cereal and banana?'

His heart soared at the first real smile she'd given him for over a year. 'Yes, so long as the bananas are ripe enough. Come on, let's see.' He led the way into the kitchen, resisting the urge to do anything stupid like touching her, no matter how badly he wanted to, or how easily he could make her want it. He'd made too many mistakes with her, it seemed.

He just wished he knew what all his mistakes were, so he didn't repeat them. Now she was finally back where she belonged, he couldn't afford to blow it again.

'How ripe is ripe enough?'

He hid the grin this time; she sounded as touchy as anxious, hating it that he knew more about babies than she did. 'They need to be soft and sweet, but not bruised. Don't worry, Anna, we can steam an apple if the bananas are too hard or soft.'

'They're all spotted—that's overripe,' Anna grumbled over the screams, rocking the baby on her hip in a futile attempt to soothe her. 'What else can go wrong today?'

'Don't worry.' Jared grabbed a red apple and a peeler. 'I've done this hundreds of times for my brothers and sisters. Five minutes and I guarantee she'll be happy.'

Anna reached up to the hanging ladder that had served as a pot rack for a century, and grabbed a small saucepan. 'How much water do you need?'

Busy peeling the apple as fast as possible, he said, 'Half an inch, and turn the heat down as soon as it's boiling. In the meantime…' He reached into his precious store of childhood favourites, his arrowroot biscuits, and handed one to Anna. 'She can have this—it's what the cereal's made of.'

She grinned as she took the semi-sweet cookie. 'You must be desperate for quiet to give up your night-time treats.'

How she managed to do insane things to his body with a grin when she looked like an extra on a horror film, he had no idea. But she did it as no other woman ever had or would, and he accepted it. She was his woman.

'Desperate,' he agreed, smiling back at her, wondering if he looked as incredibly aroused and needing as he felt. 'The kid's louder than a city street.'

'Not now,' she said softly, as the baby grabbed the arrowroot from her hand, and gurgled over the biscuit, slobbering in a chattering ecstasy only babies and children knew how to show. 'Thanks for the biscuit. It was inspired.'

He shrugged, feeling like a total idiot. She was thinking about the baby while he was thinking of how to get her into bed. 'I was the oldest of five kids. I had to mind them a lot.'

'That's a definite advantage right now.' She cocked her head towards the stove. 'The water's boiling.'

'Oh. Right.' He turned back from his rapt contemplation of the picture before him: a messy Madonna smiling for the first time in a year, holding a yabbering baby who was covered in milk and chewed biscuit. As he peeled and pared the apple and dropped slices into the water, he made a vow—he'd do whatever it took to give Anna the motherhood that had brought her back to life: the life he'd never been able to give her, despite spending over a hundred thousand on IVF implantations and specialist visits.

He'd had all his dreams come true, thanks to the Currans—especially because of Anna. He knew what he had—he'd never taken it for granted. He'd worked day and night to make life perfect for her, without the financial fears that had turned his mum grey before her time, and sent his father into the downward spiral that ended with a noose and debts that had taken him, Jared, ten years to pay off.

Even when her fertility problems meant frequent trips to Perth and massive cheques to cover the treatments, he'd made sure Anna was never burdened with the feelings of negativity and fear that his dad had pushed on his mum. Anna had never once had to worry where the next meal was coming from or how they'd pay the next round of bills, as his mum had had to for as long as he could remember.

But somehow all his hard work, everything he'd done to make their lives secure hadn't been enough to make her happy or want to stay with him. And worse still, he couldn't see how to make this fantastic life, the only life he wanted, enough for a woman like Anna.

No. I'll find the way. I'll make her happy this time. I'll work harder, tell any lie, even play daddy to this kid, if it keeps that smile on her face.

'Can you find the strainer?' he asked abruptly. Hiding the emotion as she'd accused, yeah, but at least he didn't carry on like his father had, dumping all his problems and feelings onto her. He still remembered the way Mum had tried to shut Dad up at the dinner table. *Not in front of the children, Rob!* He still remembered the low-voiced arguments over money at night, his mother's weary *Well, what do you want me to do, Rob, wave a magic wand for you?,* and his father's alternate pleading love and despairing coldness.

A family with cracks in it as wide as the dried-out red land before the Wet, the Wests had patched it together with more children, more bank loans, until the shaky edifice had collapsed around them. Then his dad had taken the easy way out. Overwhelmed with the sudden load alone, Mum had asked Bryce to take him; the next oldest, Sam, had gone to their grandparents. She raised the three little ones, Nick, Andie and Dale at his Aunty Pat's place in Perth until she'd sold off enough of the pieces of Mandurah they'd still owned to buy a house in the suburbs.

Now his mother was coming back, Nick and this bloke she was marrying coming with her.

'Why do you need a strainer?' Anna broke into his morbid reverie, her tone like his mother's had been, withdrawn and hard.

Damn, he'd done it again, broken the fragile accord just as she'd started to smile at him at last—either that or she really hated knowing nothing about babies.

If there was one thing he knew, it was that once a fence was broken completely, all you could do was build a new one from scratch. He'd broken their marriage somehow. Now he had to build their relationship over again…and this time it would be made to last. He'd build it with drought-proof, fireproof materials.

So she thought he sucked at communication?

Fix it. Talk to her. 'Mum always strained the fruit and cereal, until the kids were walking.'

She opened a drawer and handed the strainer to him without a word.

He squashed the apple through the sieve into the bowl with the mixed cereal and made-up formula, and stirred the concoction. The baby was making protesting noises again and he shoved the bowl at Anna. 'Get this mush into her and fast. She's starving, I think.'

'I doubt John or Ellie would hear much of anything, even if she wasn't hard of hearing,' Anna said dryly, pointing out the window, where a *boom* of thunder followed hard after a sheet of lightning wide enough to split the house in two. 'Looks like we got here just in time.'

Great. He wanted to prove they could communicate, and they were already reduced to talking about the weather. 'I'll make dinner while you feed her.'

'You can cook?' The faint emphasis on *you* was almost an insult…or was it teasing?

She hasn't teased me for so long…

Already heading for the fridge, he twisted around to grin at her. 'I'm a man of many talents— so long as you like scrambled eggs and bacon on toast, or omelette and chips with some salad.'

The ready laugh told him she'd actually been teasing him—then she hastily put another spoonful into the baby's mouth when she protested. 'That's something I didn't know about you.'

'I can also do a mean barbecue at a pinch,' he added, revelling in hearing her voice again, angling for her laugh. An awkward, high-pitched giggle with a tiny snort at the end, *ee-yaw*, like a donkey, it was infectious, making him laugh just to hear it.

And it came again, making him chuckle. 'Well, I'm no top chef, so we might resort to your barbecues, omelettes and salad until we can let Mrs Button back in the house.'

Elated by a stupid conversation about cooking, he swept a mock-bow. 'So which is your pleasure this evening, my lady?'

Anna stared, blinked; her mouth opened a little in pure surprise—and there was something else there, too—a touch of the sensual woman he'd refused to believe she'd buried with Adam, which was why he'd come to Broome and taken her by storm.

'What?' he asked huskily.

She shrugged, her cheeks tinged with pink. She'd either read his mind or she wanted him, too—and he chose to believe the latter. 'I haven't heard you make a joke in a long time.' Lifting the baby onto one hip, she said, 'I'll get this one bathed and to bed. She looks exhausted.'

So simple teasing and laughter made her want him? If he'd known at the start that was what she'd wanted, he'd have made her laugh constantly. But he could do it from now on...

Then he looked at the baby. She was yawning and rubbing her eyes a lot, considering she'd slept the entire trip home—and a memory stirred. 'She's either not a good traveller or she's teething—probably teething.'

Anna blinked. 'How would—?' She rolled her eyes. 'Don't tell me, your mum always said it when the kids were grumpy, right?'

He waved a pot at her. 'Don't knock my mum, it's the only source of baby information we've got right now.' *Unless you want to ask Lea*, he almost said but didn't. Some time in the years they'd lost babies and Lea had had one, Anna had turned her sister into the competition, even believing he'd wanted Lea. He might not know much about women, but one thing he was good at was knowing when to keep his mouth closed.

He was glad he'd kept quiet when, alight with laughter and mock-fear, she backed off, one hand up in surrender. 'Okay, okay, you and your mum are the fount of all baby knowledge. I worship at your feet.'

'Oh, if only,' he retorted, a hand over his heart in playful teasing to hide how much he meant it. He'd always loved the way she'd looked at him as if he was the closest thing to perfection she'd ever find. Thinking he'd never see it again—or that she'd found him out for the fraud he was— had brought the inner darkness spinning up from a buried corner of his mind, until the savagery overtook him and, desperate for relief, he had to see her, to touch her—

Anna stilled, looking at him with a depth of doubt that shook him to his soul. It made him want to run a million miles—or bolt into her arms and tell her—

Yeah, tell her what? When did you ever say the right thing?

It seemed to him he only got it right with Anna when he communicated without words.

Go slow, or you'll lose her again.

Failure was not an option—but his craving body was taking to common sense with a battle axe and battering ram, breaking down pathetic defences. Screaming, *Take her to bed and love her into submission. You know she wants to...or you can soon make her want to.*

Then the baby gave a mighty belch, and the moment broke; they burst out laughing. 'Oh, what a good girl,' Anna crooned, her face flushed as she caressed the baby's spiky hair.

Yeah, she was far from ready to touch him, by her body language—he had to play it smart here. So he grinned again. 'Isn't it funny the way we tell babies they're good when they burp or fart, and then tell them to stop it by the time they're about two?'

'Better out than in, I always say.' She chuckled. Her face buried in the baby's soft skin, he still saw her smile, and it was infectious. 'I'll be back in time for dinner—I hope.'

Jared decided on a barbecue at that moment. The uncertainty in her voice showed her confidence levels on bathing a slippery, soapy baby. He might not have bathed a baby in a long time, but he knew the basics—he could help her while the meat defrosted in the microwave. Anything that brought them together, kept them talking, was good right now—even a baby he didn't want coming between them.

He threw a salad together first, giving her five

minutes to undress the baby and run the bath. Then he went into the bathroom and Anna joined him at that moment with a naked, grumpy baby on her hip, a bottle of baby shampoo in the other hand. 'What are you doing in here?'

Her tone was cold, almost suspicious. He didn't let it get to him, but held out his arms. 'I've done this hundreds of times. Everyone needs one lesson at baby-bathing in their lifetime,' he said with a grin that felt dogged even to him. 'My mother watched over me about ten times before she trusted me not to kill the kids.'

She didn't laugh; the suspicion in her eyes dissipated a touch, but she frowned, and the watchfulness remained. 'All right,' was her only response. She handed the baby over to him as if yielding up buried treasure. Everything in her body language was screaming, *Mine*.

If laughter was the best medicine, as people said, it seemed their relationship was sick enough to need it in five-minute doses. And right up until the day she'd left him, he'd thought everything, apart from her trouble having babies, was perfect for them.

Had he been so totally blind to her unhappiness? He'd thought her only unhappiness lay in needing a child…

He put the baby in the four inches of water, leaving her sitting up. 'When they're really little you have to put your hand around and under them, holding them by the shoulder so they don't go under, but…' He frowned for a second, then remembered the baby's name and added, 'Melanie's old enough to sit, so it's easiest to make this playtime for her. You need toys and stuff to distract her while you wash, or she'll scream her way through it.'

'I know,' she said so dryly he knew she'd had a bad time of it at least once. How many times had Rosie left the baby alone with Anna?

He tried not to laugh at her tone, and failed dismally—and he was relieved when she laughed with him.

He was still chuckling as he handed Melanie a clean flannel and an empty bottle of shower gel as playthings. At this age, anything would do—but he made a mental note to buy a rubber duckie or something in Geraldton when he flew down. 'Nobody's born knowing this, you know. Not even women.'

A look crossed her face, gone so quickly he almost thought he'd imagined it—but he knew he hadn't. What had he said to put such pain in her eyes? Did she think she ought to know about babies by instinct? She'd always been able to laugh at her failures before, but Adam's death had changed something fundamental in her. He only wished he knew how to heal her of whatever it was—he needed his wife back, in his bed, his arms, in his life.

Melanie pushed the washcloth in her mouth, tasting it, chewing on it while she tried to make sense of the shower gel cap. He knew he only had a minute to show Anna what to do before the baby tired of the toys and yelled the place down. 'So you have to juggle,' he said, rushing the words as he tried to remember what he hadn't done since he'd been about fourteen. 'Pour some of the shampoo in one hand, and keep the bottle out of reach.' He put it on the sink. 'Then use your free hand to hold her by one shoulder or her back. You have to leave her hands free to play or she won't be happy.' He massaged the baby's scalp. 'Try not to rub too hard because the baby's head isn't closed yet.'

Smothered laughter made him turn his head to mock-glare at her. 'What?' he demanded, in faked indignation. It was working, she was laughing again, that crazy, infectious giggle that lit up his world…

Her eyes were bright with mirth. 'Her *head's* closed, Jared—her skull isn't.'

He rolled his eyes, keeping his hands on the baby. 'Semantics, shemantics.'

She grinned at him. 'Just keep teaching, O Yoda of babies.'

Satisfied that he'd injected more medicine into their sick—*not dead*—relationship, he turned his attention back to the task at hand, putting up with the baby's yells of protest as he laid her back and rinsed her hair so he didn't get soap in her eyes. He sat her back up with her makeshift toys as soon as he could. The rain was hissing down outside, making drumming thunder on the tin roof, but he couldn't risk the noise for long. The rain at the start of the Wet could be spasmodic, coming and going at will—and if the Buttons heard Melanie, all Anna's dreams could become toast. 'You can use the shampoo as baby soap for the rest of her, if Rosie didn't pack any.'

Anna frowned, and ran into the bedroom to check the bag. 'Here. Non-soap baby cleanser, but how you clean without soap in it I don't know.'

'Soap dries out babies' skin,' he explained without thinking.

'Fine.' She waved an irritable hand, closing the subject. 'What else?'

Melanie had worked out the gel bottle mechanism, and was gurgling in delight as she sprayed out the last of the purple gel into the water, and over her plump little legs, kicking and squealing at her achievement. They both laughed, and he knew Anna was caught between sweetness and regret, just as he was. No matter how she wanted to believe they were opposites, in their grief they were one. They were both thinking, *This could have been Adam...*

They could have been laughing together over their son's baby pride.

'We won't be fed until midnight at this rate,' he said gruffly. He squeezed the non-soap cleanser into his palm, and rubbed it all over the baby's soft skin, rinsing her with a cupped hand over and over. Then he lifted her wriggling, slippery form into the air, dripping water. 'Hand me a towel.'

Anna wrapped the fluffy soft towel around the baby, taking her into her arms as if she couldn't wait to claim her rights. 'Thanks, Jared. I can take it from here.'

Hating being locked out, he tried to think of a new way to be useful. 'How many nappies do you have left? How much cereal?'

The sudden panic in her eyes made him rush to reassure her. 'I can fly up to a petrol station, or go to Geraldton or Kununurra tomorrow if you're almost out.'

Given reprieve yet again, Anna tried to think as she carried Melanie through to the bedroom she'd used for seven months, since moving out of Jared's bed until she'd left. 'I think I have about a quarter left—it was a pack of fifty—but the cereal's almost gone. I don't think the service station will have everything—and you know old Ernie, he's Stop One on the Bush Telegraph Gossip connection.'

'Good point…and too many people know us in Geraldton. Kununurra it is, then. I probably won't be back in time to give her the cereal, but you can mush up the arrowroot in the morning with the formula. I'll take off early. I'll steam an apple for you before I go.'

'Thanks, Jared.' Again she felt relief. She didn't know what she'd have done without him today. They'd worked together as a team. If that was the point he was trying to make, he'd done it magnificently. 'I'll have lunch ready when you're back,' she offered as she dried the baby, tickling her between to hear that silvery laugh, like sweet, tinkling bells.

'Speaking of food, I'll go start the barbecue.'

His voice was husky again, and she realised he'd been watching the curve of her butt as she'd worked. She flushed again, feeling tension replace the accord: the tension he'd probably misconstrue as sexual, because he still didn't seem to have any idea why she'd left. 'Good idea.'

He left the room. She didn't watch him go or look at the long, clean lines of him, a strong working man of the land. The ache of feminine yearning was strong whenever she was near him, and when he smiled at her like that—but walking right alongside the physical, sexual desire was the sense of utter uselessness. Why bother with an act that might bring temporary joy, but could only reinforce what she no longer was, what she'd never be again? He couldn't even truly want her now, surely—this was about keeping Jarndirri, keeping his word. She wasn't a real woman any more; she was an empty shell, a hulk of a car without its engine.

A woman is far more than her womb, Anna, she's a man's other half, the gentleness, the empathy. A man needs a woman for far more than babies alone. The counsellor Jared had paid an exorbitant amount to fly up here every week to let her talk had sprouted those and many other glib words, but they'd brought no comfort or healing, only more unspoken resentment. How could any woman who hadn't lost both her only child and her last chance of having children at the same time understand the word *empty*, and how much it encompassed?

She had to make Jared give up on her, and find someone who could give him what he needed. So she didn't watch him move; she fought the desire with everything in her.

Motherhood by proxy she could do. But how could she be a wife again, a *woman*, when she felt like a blank slate, almost androgynous? No, she wasn't that good an actress. She knew what Jared wanted—far more than sex alone, he wanted what he'd had, a wife and partner in Jarndirri—but it was impossible. He was the man who reminded her of everything she'd once been…and never could be again. Desire and endless grief in one taut, man-of-the-land body…

When she entered the kitchen she found a fresh, warm bottle waiting. She fed Melanie one last time, and the baby was fast asleep within a minute. Anna rocked her, softly crooning long after she knew Melanie couldn't hear her. Ah, motherhood was so sweet, even by proxy.

She laid Melanie in the bassinette she'd just about outgrown, and placed it on the middle of the queen spare bed, surrounding her once again with all the pillows she could find, making a safe zone with every chair in the house. It meant they'd have to eat on the verandah, but that was a good thing: she knew Ellie and John Button would be watching. It also meant some touching, even some kissing to prove their reconciliation was real.

Her fingers curled hard over one of the chair backs. *You can handle this. Do it for Rosie, and for Melanie.*

The wafting smell of steak and onions came to her, and her stomach reminded her how long it had been since she'd had more than coffee. She walked out the door to the back verandah, where Jared, shirt plastered to his chest from Melanie's kick-ups of water, was flipping the meat onto a platter already laden with onions. 'I hope you're hungry.'

'Starving, actually,' she confessed, with an uneven laugh. He looked so—so like every dream she'd had since she'd been fifteen—and he knew how to bring her every desire to life.

To divert herself from her fast-growing obsession, she reached for the platter, taking the food to the outdoor setting where the salad and dressings lay waiting. 'I guess we eat out here, since all the chairs are surrounding Melanie's bed...'

Her words dried up as she looked at him. She'd put Melanie in her bed, in the room that had been hers in childhood, and again after she'd moved out of their marital bed. There were many other rooms with beds here, but the implication—

'I need a mattress put on the floor in her room,' she said quickly, putting the plate down so he wouldn't see her hands shaking. So he wouldn't see how much she wanted and ached for what she craved, but shouldn't have again. 'It's her first night in a new place. She'll need someone familiar beside her if she wakes.'

'It's her second new place in a week, too, which is probably also why she was so unsettled tonight,' he replied, his gaze penetrating, but his tone was calm. 'I'll bring one in for you when you're ready to sleep.'

Glad she wasn't facing him, she wet her lips. 'Thank you.' What else to say? He seemed so helpful, so strong, and so able to resist her...and though it should reassure her, it only unsettled her. When he'd come to her in Broome, it had been her place, her say. Now, even though she was half-owner of Jarndirri, she felt as if she'd lost her sense of power. He'd taken control again—he was master of her future, as well as her desires.

And yet he'd done nothing but help since she'd entered the house.

'So tell me about life here since…in the past few months,' she said with overdone carelessness. Telling him not to get too personal or come too close without words.

He shrugged, but smiled, and she realised it was the first time she'd asked anything about Jarndirri since her time in hospital. 'It's all going as normal. The seasons have been pretty good this year, behaving themselves nicely. The crop was excellent, and we got good prices for the beef and lamb. Stock from the neighbouring properties have wandered in, and we mustered them and took them back. One or two sheep have drowned in the river, two cows have died calving.'

'The round of farming life,' she replied, hearing the slight dreaminess in her voice. 'I noticed my veggie patch is still thriving. I thought it'd be long gone.'

He turned his face toward the murky grey of the rain and falling darkness behind the thick curtain of clouds. 'It's a good place to shovel the muck from the stables, and the plants seem to do well with it. Watering doesn't take long.'

With a little start, she blinked at him. 'You're the one who's been looking after it?'

He frowned almost fiercely. 'Why not? It's a good source of fresh food, cheaper than flying stuff in, and it solves the dung problem. It makes economic sense to take care of it.'

Funny, but though all he said was true, her mouth twitched. She got the feeling he wasn't telling the whole truth, and that wasn't like the Jared she'd always known. 'Thank you for not letting it die,' she said softly. It was a part of her.

If anything, his frown grew. 'You can take care of it again, now you're back. It'll save me an hour a day.' As he said it his gaze came back to her, lingered on her face.

'Of course,' she said quietly, still hiding a smile. 'And even if it only made good economic sense, I'm still glad you saved it.'

Strangely, as they ate, the thrumming rain on the tin roof became a companion, making the quiet somehow peaceable. She found herself smiling at her surroundings, familiar and loved throughout her life; smiling at the rain, her old friend—and she even smiled at Jared, who watched her with smoky-dark eyes, shadows of desire in the darkness. The wanting quivered in the air between them—and instead of being her enemy, her weakness, it gave odd comfort to her hurting heart. After he'd humiliated her before with *Kissing used to make you happy*, he was showing her he still wanted her…

Her smile grew and she sighed.

His voice drifted to her over the drumming beat of the Wet's fall, deep and soft, filling her soul. 'Is my barbecue that good?'

'Actually, it is,' she replied, liking even the small talk. 'What's the marinade?'

His brows lifted. 'I'd tell you, but then I'd have to kill you.'

She laughed, feeling relaxed enough—aroused enough—to slide back into the old teasing banter they'd always shared before making love. 'The man's a spy. He has to be. Everything's a state secret, from his early life to his emotions and even his barbecue sauce.'

After a moment, he chuckled, moved an inch closer to her. 'Australia has so many enemies, especially out here.'

'You have a million hectares.' She grinned at him in a playful kind of challenge she hadn't felt with him since they'd been engaged, and she'd been able to pump him for anything she'd wanted to know. 'You're hiding a nuclear power facility out here. Mining uranium to sell to the unknown enemy. Making weapons of mass destruction. Building satellite dishes to listen in on our neighbours.'

He laughed and shook his head. 'Okay, I get it. I never was big on small talk.' His fingers touched hers, and she drew in a breath as her taunt came back to mock her, *I don't want to sleep with you.*

To string out the growing warmth between

them, the certainty of shared desire, she threw him an incredulous glance. 'Now, there's the understatement of the year. You were never big on *any* talk, except to your horses.'

'I get it, Anna. I don't know how to communicate…but I'm trying. I can learn, if you'll help me out,' he said quietly, his eyes locked on hers, filled with meaning.

'I am helping. I'm saying all I want to say for now.' She sighed, and put her fork and knife down. 'I don't want to revisit emotions that are best left buried. Can't we just talk like this, Jared? Have some fun, like we used to?'

'All right,' he agreed, in a lighter tone, 'but before we descend to the weather and what groceries you want me to buy tomorrow, I have a confession.'

'Oh, this sounds exciting,' she teased to hide the sudden kick-up of her pulse. Anticipation was born and grew legs, running away with her galloping imagination. She knew what he was going to say but, oh, she wanted to hear it. 'Spill. I can hardly wait.'

He leaned toward her, that arousing half-smile coming to life as he murmured, 'I lied to you when I said I only kissed you yesterday to make you happy.' The intent look in his eyes, the hunter's trap, caught her in his sights, and she felt herself melting…

'Oh?' she managed to murmur, knowing she'd given herself away when his smile grew.

'I kissed you to make me happy,' he said, soft, purposeful, thrilling her.

'Oh,' she said again, lame, stupid, needing. The beautiful feminine pain filling her with just a few words, knowing it was going to happen. It was always inevitable; from the first time they'd made love, it had become their release, their addiction.

'I was starving for you, Anna,' he whispered, a few inches from her mouth. 'I've lived a year without you, when a day is too long for me.'

She'd lost the power to speak, and he still hadn't even touched her.

But then he reached for her—but didn't sweep her into his arms. His index finger caressed her jaw, her throat, a fingertip so light she could barely feel it, and she was gone. 'I'm still starving for you…and now you're here, I'll be doing my dead-level best to have you in my bed—tonight and every night.'

As she gasped softly and wet her lips in instinctive reaction, he leaned right to her and brushed his mouth over hers, once, twice, yet again, slower and deeper, lush and sensual as she knew only Jared could kiss her…and she couldn't find any words, no resistance inside to stop him, or to stop herself.

'Come to me,' he whispered against her mouth, and she moaned, the pleasure-pain low in her

belly flashed up, filling her from head to toe.
'Come to bed with me, love.' His fingers lightly
touched her breast, and she gasped again in unbearable excitement. She swayed into him, everything forgotten but her body's need too long
denied, screaming for release.

'Jared,' she whispered, her hands shaking as
she unbuttoned his shirt. 'Ah, Jared, what you do
to me…'

'And you to me,' he muttered, gruff, husky,
making her shiver all over. 'Now,' he whispered,
after another kiss, rough desire and hot command.

Caution and consequences were drowned in
the rain; all she could think of was here and now,
Jared's hands, mouth and body…and that beautiful big bed, only a few feet from where they sat
touching as if tomorrow wouldn't come. 'Yes,
now,' she whispered.

With that slow half-smile she adored, he swung
her up into his arms and carried her inside.

CHAPTER SIX

WHAT a night…

Jared lay on his back on the bed, holding Anna close in the aftermath of the second bout of lovemaking—both in bed and in the shower—and for the first time in over a year, he felt almost complete, nearly happy. If he'd been starving for her, she'd been just as hungry. Her hands and lips had been all over him; she hadn't been able to get enough.

He was winning her back. He was close, so close—and though it must be nearly two in the morning, she still wasn't leaving the bed. She lay tangled over him, hair damp and messy from the shower, tasting his skin with mouth and tongue.

His body leaped from sated to needing in an instant.

She'd always had that ability, from that first haystack kiss. The sexual encounters he'd had with girls he'd met at rodeos and pubs, cattle sales, parties and the infamous Bachelor & Spinster balls during his teens had been a fun diversion, but he'd never bothered using the numbers the girls had given him, or wanted to repeat the experience with the same girl. They didn't know him, knew only his looks or his name, *the* Jared West, Bryce Curran's adopted heir, expected to inherit Jarndirri. And every time he left a girl's bed, it had left him curiously blank. He'd felt empty from the moment he'd found satisfaction.

Until a single, impulsive, forbidden kiss, given because Anna had looked so adorable with hay in her hair and chocolate smears on her mouth…and instead of pulling away to demand what he was doing, she'd wrapped her arms around his neck with a little, feminine sound of surprised arousal, and had kissed him back. From that moment, like Alice down the rabbit hole, he'd fallen into a desire and need so all-encompassing that, twelve years later, he still hadn't found a way out.

No amount of waiting, from school to university and the year she'd spent teaching in the Northern Territory; no change in their lives, no loss or even her leaving him lessened the craving. Seeing her pretty, funny pixie face, her lush curves, hearing her husky voice—or even her ridiculous laugh— turned him into a burning mass of desire.

And after a long year of empty abstinence, she was here, keeping him on constant slow burn with mumbled words and lighting trails of fire with her mouth. He turned to her, lifting her face for another *I can't get enough of you* kiss. She moaned and arched into him, and they were consumed with each other again.

And with each touch and every kiss he tried to tell her everything his heart kept locked away from the world, all the little family secrets he'd never told anyone, and the overwhelming feelings he had for her.

All the emotion and pain he could never tell Anna had been communicated through the years with his fidelity and his voracious need for her—and he now prayed she understood.

Afterwards Anna yawned and stretched, smiling at him. 'Can you help me drag a mattress into Melanie's room?'

Something inside Jared stilled then withered. Okay, after so long apart he hadn't been completely expecting the words of love she'd always given after loving each other into sublime satiety, but *Can you help me move a mattress* wasn't high on his list of things he'd hoped to hear.

Anger flashed through him. 'You're staying with me.'

The smile vanished. 'I've been away from Melanie long enough. It's her first night in a strange place, as *you* pointed out. She's fast asleep now but if she wakes she could try to get out of the bassinette.'

You've been away from me far longer than enough. 'You're making excuses. She can't possibly roll off the bed with every chair in the house surrounding her—she's not that strong. And you made a deal,' he growled, hating himself for pulling a blackmail stunt on her but knowing that the longer he let her stay away, the farther her heart went from him. 'You need me if you want to adopt the kid, and in return I get what I want. You're my wife. I want you to sleep with me.'

The eyes he'd always loved looking into, like a rich, warm snugly brown blanket of love made just for him, were cold and hard. 'I just spent the past few hours giving you *what you want*. I need to check on Melanie.' She rolled over and got to her feet—and with a flash of fury at her defiance, his hand shot out and grabbed her wrist, pulling her back to the bed.

She struggled against him. 'She's not *the kid*,' she panted. 'She's the only baby I'll ever have in my life, and I will stay with her. I won't lose her the way I lost Adam because you have to win again, to own me. You wouldn't be stopping me now if it was Adam in that room!'

The bitterness inside her words turned him cold. Without thinking, he released her arm. Anna meant it. She really loved that baby—and she truly believed she would never have children of her own.

Would she ever begin to heal, come back to reality?

'This is the twenty-first century,' he said, low and fierce, yet with a sense of feeling his way. 'There are a dozen other ways to have babies—'

'Not for me.' Flat, angry words, with an underlying certainty that haunted him. 'You don't understand. You'll never understand.'

Her ire roused his. 'I understand that you gave me your word today, and you're already breaking it. I'm doing my part. I keep my promises.'

Her lips pressed together, so hard they were rimmed with white. 'I'll be back in a minute.'

Totally naked, she walked out of the room, and he heard the door opening to the room where the baby slept. He heard her croon softly to the kid, her voice rich with long-thwarted mother-love. Then, in exactly a minute, she returned and lay back down on the bed, but she remained rolled away from him, letting him know without words how little she wanted to be there, even after making love three times. Every pore and cell of her screamed, *Don't touch me*.

He'd never been very good at taking orders— and not touching her wasn't something he was prepared to negotiate. He pulled her against him, loving the lush curves of her body against him after so long away…and he'd be willing to bet she loved it, too, despite her silent resistance.

But when she only lay stiff and cold against him, refusing to touch him voluntarily, and her breathing was uneven, choppy as she chewed on her anger and fear that the longer she stayed away, the higher the risk the baby would be hurt, Jared knew he'd made an enormous mistake. Lying beside his wife, holding her naked body close, he discovered anew a distance far greater than anything that could be measured in kilometres.

Seducing her had seemed the perfect solution only a few hours before. Making love had always brought them closer. In the loving and its aftermath, she poured out her affection, her love for him, as well as showing him the hidden tigress when they touched.

Tonight all he'd seen had been the sensual woman. His body was sated, but his heart was empty. He'd gambled high stakes on finding *his* Anna, the Anna he missed so badly, in bed—that she'd come back to him in the loving—and he'd lost, big time.

Aching for what seemed forever gone, the wife who'd loved cuddling him at night, his haven in a world gone wrong long before his father had put a rope around his neck, Jared moved his arm, giving her the choice, the freedom. Anna immediately rolled onto her stomach, finding a spare pillow to use beneath her body.

She was with him, beside him, and told him without words that it was the last place she wanted to be.

I might enjoy the sex, but that's all it will be. She'd warned him, and he'd ignored her, ploughing ahead with his own plans for victory.

Maybe it was time he started not just asking but listening to her.

'Go back to the baby.' It was a rough growl filled with anger, but it was surrender. It was listening to her, giving her more than he'd ever had to before. 'I'll bring the mattress in.'

She rolled back to face him, staring at him in obvious surprise—and after a moment's searching glance, her mouth curved in a tiny smile. 'Thank you.'

It was far from the *'I love you'* he'd once taken for granted as his right, his due, and now craved to hear; but he'd take it—a smile was a step in the right direction.

Yeah, it looked like it was definitely time he started listening to what she was actually saying, not what he thought she wanted—and he'd watch her body language. If he got really lucky, maybe she'd seduce him next time, and stay because she wanted to.

Her strong, curvaceous working woman's body made him ache again as she gathered her scattered clothes and made a beeline for the bathroom—but he'd made a forward step, and he wasn't about to blow it.

As he dragged the mattress into the other room for her, finding space for it in a corner beside the plethora of chairs she'd used for the baby's safety, he wondered how he could have made so many mistakes with her and missed them—and how he'd lost her love without even noticing when it had gone missing.

Unfamiliar shame washed through Anna when she'd awoken with Melanie's cries at seven the next morning to find a bottle made ready in the kitchen, apples steamed and strained for the baby and already mashed through his arrowroots. He'd even left coffee hot in the pot.

He'd made everything for her before he'd flown out, so all she had to do this morning was bond with Melanie. After her ungracious refusal to stay with him—which she guessed he probably had the right to expect after making love three times— he'd still kept his word.

The plane moved slowly into the hangar again at eleven, during Melanie's morning nap. 'Can you help me unpack the gear, Anna?' he yelled over the beat of the rain.

'Coming.' She ran out to the hangar, drenched before she made it into the massive double doors. She blinked in surprise when she saw the plane stacked to the roof. 'What's all that you've got there?'

Opening the back doors of the plane with care, Jared grinned at her, his black hair plastered to his forehead just by the twenty seconds he'd been outside calling for her. And the brightness of his eyes, that slow, sure smile sent her insides into silly flips. How did he still do that to her after all these years? 'I brought back lunch and dinner from the pub in Kununurra,' he said, 'meat pies and chips to reheat in the oven, and a lasagne with garlic bread for dinner.'

She frowned. 'You went to the pub?'

He kept smiling at her. 'Don't worry about gossip. The tom-toms are already out on us. I got a call outside the grocery store from Jim Turner's missus. She wanted to feed us to say welcome home to you, and happy second honeymoon.'

'The Turners didn't see the nappies and cereal?' she asked anxiously.

He flipped her concern away with a hand. 'I got a tourist lady to buy them—she thought it was hilarious that I couldn't be seen buying baby stuff. She made some joke about a woman's underwear department. I didn't get it.'

'I do.' Anna heard herself chuckling. Crazy that, after all these years, Jared had found a new ability to make her laugh, even when he had her thinking about second honeymoons and all they entailed…

Jared shrugged and grinned, willing to be the butt of humour; the thin, wet cotton shirt stretched taut across his shoulders and back as he bent into the plane to pick something up, and her mouth dried with ridiculous longing. How pathetic was it that she could want him again so badly, only hours after they'd spent half the night making love?

'We can't get too many baby things yet,' he was saying, his voice muffled. 'It'll look too suspicious—but…' A smile of boyish excitement filled his eyes with sapphire brilliance as he turned back to her, opening something. *'Voilà!'*

Anna's jaw dropped—unbelievably, he'd brought a collapsible travel cot!

'Where did you get that?' she asked, awed and a little worried. If the store owner remembered him later… Then she noticed its slightly rusty legs.

He laughed, his normally in-control face, like a carving of Alexander the Great, was alight with teasing pride. 'Would you believe it? I saw it left by the road near the airstrip. It's a bit busted up, but I'll fix it before she needs to sleep tonight. It's wet, but it's all plastic coated so all we have to do is wipe it down. I bought a few thin pillows to use as a mattress for her. So you don't need to worry about her safety. The baby's got a bed.'

Anna had had to swallow a lump in her throat.

This wasn't the man she'd married. Her Jared would never have noticed a collapsible cot, let alone stopped to get it.

Or maybe he would. He'd saved the lives of two kids by diving into a swollen, raging river, had flown through dangerous storms to help others.

Flown through thunderclouds to reach her in the time he'd promised.

He'd found the cot for her. The way he didn't even call Melanie by name told her how little he wanted to bond with a baby that wasn't his. But he'd gone to all this trouble to make her happy. Even if he'd done it to keep her in bed with him, to stop her from needing to sleep with the baby, he'd still made Melanie more comfortable.

She should have known he'd do it. Whatever she'd ever given him, Jared had always found ways to return it tenfold. *That* was her Jared, the man who moved heaven and earth to keep a promise, or risked his own life to help others.

Just don't ask him to talk, she reminded herself ironically.

He's talking now, isn't he? an imp in her mind taunted her. *You're the one refusing to open up...*

'I can't believe you managed all this without anyone noticing,' she said as they kept unstacking. 'But I'm not really surprised. You always did come up with brilliant plans.'

After a short silence, he shrugged. 'We'll have

to wait until after dark to bring in the baby supplies. You know how curious Mrs Button can be.'

'Good plan.' She refused to create new unspoken tension between them, after all the debacles yesterday. Him being away had given her time to think. The adoption authorities would want to see a happy, loving couple here, not tense silences and discord, if she wanted any hope of keeping Melanie. She had to keep things light and happy. 'Thank you,' she said as she helped him unpack the plane. 'I really appreciate it.'

He glanced outside then moved on her, so close she could smell the honest sweat on him, taste the desire he never wanted to hide from her. Her body, already stirring in response to his wet shirt, flared to life with the touch of his cool skin in the watery heat. 'There's a better way to thank me, one I think we'd both enjoy.' He lifted her face and kissed her, hard and hungry.

Before she knew it her hands were in his hair. Cooling heated palms on the raindrops running through it; she moved against him, with a soft sound of exultation and need.

They kissed until they both forgot where they were, slowly dropping to the ground, undressing each other with trembling fingers. Jared was lying on her, and she gloried in the feel of his taut body on hers, the hard arousal—

Suddenly an alert went off in her mind. What

was she doing—again? The more she gave in to this, the more right he had to hope she wouldn't leave. And things would go back to the way they'd always been. A hard life, a satisfying life, loving the land and the work, but...

She pushed him away an inch. 'I've got to go in to Melanie,' she said softly, kissing him once more so he didn't think she was angry or withdrawing from him. He'd done so much for her. 'She'll be waking soon.'

Expecting some curt or cutting words about Melanie and her priorities, she almost started when he smiled at her again and helped her to her feet. 'Put the oven on when you go in, will you? Lunch needs reheating. I'll find a way to get these things in under cover before Ellie Button dies of curiosity.'

Anna blinked and shook her head. 'Is this an alien abduction? Who is this man who actually seems to want to talk, and when will you take me to your leader?'

He bent and kissed her again, his chuckle making her lips vibrate. 'From James Bond to *My Husband Is An Alien*—what's the next Hollywood comparison?'

'I think that alien was a stepmother,' she whispered back, the soft, breathy laugh touching his lips as his touched hers. The shock sent tingling through her, but it was a pleasant, sensual vibration. She might barely recognise this Jared, but whoever this man was she—*liked* him.

Shaken by the thought, she turned away from him, gathered the lunch sack and dinner basket under each arm, drew a deep breath and bolted through the sheets of water to the house. She needed space, distance from this new, fun, exciting Jared. Wanting him she could handle; but liking and wanting him at once was dangerously close to emotions that could see her walking voluntarily back into the Jarndirri cage.

She could never go back to that. A life of being what her father had wanted, what Jared had wanted, instead of what *she* wanted. Subjugating herself to suit the men in her life, the life even strong-minded Lea couldn't take—no, she couldn't live like that any more. She'd never be that lost, needing woman again.

She ran through the back door, soaking wet in fifty metres, to hear Melanie's voice through the open bedroom door. The baby wasn't crying; she was making *blah-blah-blah*, singsong sounds.

Melanie seemed remarkably resilient to strangers, happy to go with her. If Rosie didn't change her mind, Melanie could be happy with her…

Grabbing the opportunity while the baby was happy, she put lunch in the oven, turned it on and ran to the bathroom to dry off the water running in rivulets down her skin. Despite the happy play, she couldn't risk Melanie getting bored, crawling out of her bassinette and rolling off the bed. The sooner that travel cot was ready, the better.

'She seems a happy baby,' Jared said as he joined her in the bathroom nearest the main bedroom, the one that had always been theirs.

She snapped back, her face muffled in a towel, 'Why shouldn't she be?'

Then she felt ashamed. Why had an innocuous remark instantly put her on the defensive?

Though he said nothing at first, Jared's gaze burned right through the towel to make her cheeks heat up. 'No reason,' was all he said, his tone light yet penetrating, and what he'd left unsaid hung in the air between them like an accusation. *Don't get your hopes up. Don't forget Rosie could change her mind.*

She hung up the towel, but still didn't look at him. Her recent discovery of new feelings for the man she thought she knew was too raw, too frightening to keep thinking about. 'I'll grab her while you set the table.'

'I need to— Sure,' he amended, and she knew he'd seen her stiffen. 'Can you help me feed the animals and shovel out the muck this afternoon?'

'Of course I can.' Then she frowned. 'But what do we do with Melanie?'

'The cot's portable, remember? There are also some of yours and Lea's kiddie toys in the attic.

I'll grab them before we go out. She should be happy enough being in sight of us—and she might like the animals too. Most babies do.'

'Good thought.' They'd both been exposed to farm animals before they'd been able to sit up, put on ponies before their first birthdays. If Melanie was going to live here—

She skidded to a shocked mental halt. That wasn't and never would be the plan, no matter what Jared believed, or made deals over. She'd make sure he didn't want her to stay…then she could find a life of her own at last, and he'd be free. 'I'll get her,' she said curtly, and walked out before he could say anything else to set her *thinking*.

Melanie was chewing on a pillow, grabbing others and dropping them, laughing in baby delight at her accomplishments.

When she saw Anna coming for her, she gurgled and lifted her arms—and Anna's heart flipped with joy and tenderness. Yes, superimposed over Melanie's beautiful dimpled face was, maybe always would be, Adam's, but she was a beautiful girl in her own right, and deserved a mother's love as much as Anna craved to give it.

Don't get your hopes up…

Sometimes in the past year she'd thought about having children by other means, such as adoption—but part of her kept believing that she couldn't possibly love a child not of her own body as she'd loved Adam. Would she resent that poor child more than she'd love them?

That worry, and the deeper knowledge that she couldn't put another set of parents through the anguish of loss had held her back from giving in to the darkest temptation when she'd seen a baby outside a store in a pram, looking so alone and neglected...

'Thank God I didn't know,' she whispered as she gathered Melanie's warm limbs into her arms, cuddling her close. 'Thank God.'

'For what?'

She stilled for a moment, fury filling her for him thinking he had the right to come on her in this private moment. Even worse was the knowledge that her promise *gave* him that right. *Whatever he wants...*

The air crackled with expectation—his and hers. Pivotal moments came to every marriage. She could keep playing the good girl, or be a woman and tell the truth.

'For Melanie,' she said quietly as she laid the baby down to change her nappy, giving herself a minute to change her mind. The baby's romper pants were wet as well, so she rubbed Melanie down with baby wipes before putting on a nappy and clean clothing.

When she was done, he was still waiting for the

rest in his usual silence. It seemed that, at last, he really wanted to know.

So she added with deliberation, 'For not knowing until she came into my life that I could love another child this deeply.' She turned on him in slow defiance. 'If I'd known before she came to me that I could feel such love for any baby but Adam, I might have done the unthinkable.'

And surely that should shock conventional Jared into letting her fall from the cursed Curran pedestal he kept her on.

But to her surprise, he nodded slowly. 'I saw it in your eyes yesterday, the guilt. I've been thanking God ever since then for watching out for you when I didn't.'

It shocked her to her core that perfectionist Jared had not only seen the truth but understood her unbearable temptation, and forgiven her. If she didn't shore up her defences, and fast, she'd never leave this place again—and she couldn't gamble her life, and Melanie's, on Jared's changes becoming soul-deep, or that they'd be permanent.

Willing away the softening of her heart, she lifted her chin. 'You're not responsible for me, Jared. I left you, remember? I make my own decisions now.'

Instead of withdrawing, as he had every time she'd reminded him that as far as she was concerned they were still separated, he looked deep into her eyes and said, 'I keep my vows.'

It should have moved her, filled her with love…words like that had always turned her into a shivering mass of loving woman. But this time all she felt was driving anger. *Keep your cool…* 'Selectively,' she replied, coolness in the single word, and she walked past him. 'Lunch must be just about ready.'

His voice came from behind her as she strode through the house, dark and, yes, finally, withdrawn. 'You don't need to remind me of my selective vow-keeping. It comes to me every night in my dreams. Losing Adam because I listened to the midwife, not you…you lying in that pool of blood the next day…and whose fault it was that it all happened. I know, Anna. I know.'

Arrested by the tone, she wheeled around to frown at him. He hadn't used the amused reproof that always made her feel small, or the enigmatic coldness that made her wither inside. Every word he'd spoken had been aimed inward. Self-recrimination wasn't something she was used to from Jared. He was Action Man, always finding the way out, always saving the day. 'What?' she spluttered as he pushed past her to get the pies and chips from the oven. 'You blame yourself for what happened? You think I blame you for…?'

'Who else is there to blame?' He pulled out

plates and put the food on them, got cutlery from the drawer. He didn't look at her. 'You do, too, Anna, or you'd never have left. You wouldn't have moved out of our bed if some part of you didn't believe me at least partly responsible for Adam's death, and your near-death.'

Beyond shock now—how many years had she wanted Jared to say something so profound, and *ask* her?—she opened her mouth, but nothing came out. *Did* she blame him for that?

At that moment Melanie lunged forward, trying to get to the floor, and she let the baby down, where she happily tugged at a broken corner of black-and-white linoleum that needed replacement. Anna replaced the makeshift toy with a wooden spoon, which Melanie began banging with a gurgle.

Then Anna found her mouth moving of its own accord, words she didn't know were true or a lie. 'Jared, I never once thought—'

'Don't say it, Anna. If you're going to leave me after this, despite your promise, then at least end it honestly,' he said with suppressed violence. 'Our son is dead because of me.'

Thunder cracked overhead, and the baby jumped; her face crumpled, and she wailed. Glad of the distraction, Anna touched her downy little head in a loving caress of reassurance, but her mind had stalled like a car engine that had run out of oil. 'What do you want me to say?' she asked slowly, feeling that pivotal moment stretching out, unwinding like a ball of yarn.

'It's not about what I want,' he said, with a dark unutterable weariness that tugged at her soul. 'For once in our lives, stop playing Miss Perfect, stop giving me what I want and tell me the truth.'

The truth was that, for months, she'd hated the world for not understanding, hated the help group that she'd attended for having found a place of peace she hadn't been able to see. She'd hated Lea for having Molly so easily and so carelessly from a one-night stand, hated Jared for getting on with life when she couldn't, didn't know how—didn't want to.

This was why she'd hated those she loved the most—for never asking—and at last he'd asked, at the perfect moment. The perfect time for him.

She gave a tired laugh. 'Oh, that's great, Jared, ask when it's less painful, less imperative, when I have Melanie, and I don't feel as if I'm bleeding to death any more.' Her hands curled into balls, shaking, longing to lash out. 'You didn't want to know before, you *ignored* me when I all but begged you to hear me, so why choose now, when it can't make a difference?'

He stood with his back to her, legs spread wide, his white-knuckled hands gripping the kitchen bench like he stood in quicksand and it stopped him sinking. 'Because I'm not too afraid to ask you now.'

'Because you're back on home territory, and in control?' she half mocked, the months of repressed fury and *betrayal* bubbling up in unexpected flashpoint.

As if he'd expected the words, he shrugged and said simply, 'Because I've already lost you, lost Adam. So say it, Anna; get it all out. There can't be worse.'

On legs surprisingly steady—maybe part of her had always known he'd ask eventually; he'd been waiting for this time, when he was back safe on his turf—she found a chair and sat down, half-facing Melanie, replacing the flooring corner which she was pulling at again with a plastic bottle. The baby began banging it on the floor, squealing in delight at the juddering noise.

And, watching the baby, she felt the fury draining away, just when she wanted to hold hard to it. With a little sigh, she let her heart speak for her. 'Why did you never even hesitate about choosing to implant Adam when the doctor said it was dangerous to try again? *Why*, Jared? He'd told us fairly bluntly that the baby and I could both die, but you kept pushing. Was a son worth more to you than my life?'

After a long silence, broken only by Melanie's play, he asked, 'Are you hungry? Lunch will get cold soon.'

There it was, his withdrawal, right on cue. Don't poke and prod me like a cow, don't push me or I'll retreat. It was her turn now to make it easy, to say yes and eat, and after the baby was asleep he'd reward her in the way that had once made her happy, had once been enough.

It had *never* been enough.

She lifted her chin, and spoke from a place of control, because she no longer *cared* if he retreated or withheld affection from her. 'No, I'm not hungry. I asked you a question, and I'd like you to answer it.'

He stopped in mid-stride, turning to stare at her from over his shoulder. 'Have you believed that all this time?' His face was unreadable, but his voice held some deeper-hidden emotion.

'Stop it,' she said, soft, holding in the anger lest they upset the baby. 'Stop turning the questions onto me. You always do that instead of answering, to make me talk. It's your way of finding out *my* issue so you can find the solution to the problem.'

He wheeled right around to face her then, frowning. 'You don't *want* a solution?'

The question was so typically Jared, she laughed before turning his words of the day before onto him. 'I want you to talk.' Then, in deliberate provocation, she added, 'I want you to have the courage to answer my question.'

His clenched fist thudded on the sink. 'I don't know what I'm supposed to say.'

The confusion, the frustration rang so clear she heard it like a bell tolling. He didn't understand, didn't know what to do if he couldn't do, couldn't act, couldn't fix. He was waiting for his cue to charge into the fray like Lancelot, finding a way to make things better.

'I asked you a question. Was having the required son and heir worth more to you than my life?' she asked again. Pushing with a rapier covered in silk.

'Dear God, how can you even ask?' he rasped.

'I need to know. I need to hear it. I've wondered—doubted—for a long time.'

He shook his head, with a slow wonder. 'I did everything for you, for us.' Anger vibrated through every word, denial of what she'd asked.

'You talked me into trying once more, with the last embryo—with Adam—when they'd told us both the risks. I was terrified, but you never faltered. You had to have your son, the Curran heir. That's how it felt to me, Jared.' She kept her voice gentle but she was pitiless. She had to know. When he didn't answer, she went on, 'I'd given you one of two things you'd planned for the life you wanted—Jarndirri—and you had to have the other, your son and heir from a Curran woman's body. If the cost was my life, it didn't seem to matter.'

In the silence, she saw a sheet of white-hot lightning rip across the sky outside the window. She lifted Melanie into her arms before the *boom* followed and frightened her. When the sound passed she put the baby down again and turned to look at him, saw his fingers clenching that old, worn bench so tightly, his fingers looked ready to snap.

Or maybe it was Jared that was about to snap.

She forced herself to not move to him, to not comfort him with touch, and do the talking for him. She'd waited too long to know.

'It mattered.' He was taut, holding onto control by a tiny thread. The struggle was so clear inside him she could almost see the straining, emotions against his will, a tug of war she'd never known existed until now, when the rope was stretched to breaking.

'But not as much as having a son—Bryce Curran's grandson, to legitimise your claim on Jarndirri,' she said softly. *Snip.*

His shoulders pulled at the shirt as the muscles moved beneath, clenching his fists over and over, thudding the bench. 'You never told me how scared you were. I thought you wanted a baby more than anything. I thought it would make you happy. You were so lost after the last time.'

Understanding flashed through her at the muttered words; they made sense. Yes, he'd wanted a son, but he'd thought it was what *she* wanted, and she hadn't told him.

It was only now she wondered: had she begun to withdraw from Jared emotionally even before Adam's death? Had she expected him to know how she felt without telling him, and then blamed him for not seeing her terror?

Tentative, unsure, she said softly, 'But when the doctor said it was dangerous, you didn't hesitate for a moment.'

He shrugged, shook his head. 'It made no sense to me. I didn't realise I'd…'

'You never knew you'd have to sacrifice anything for my sake? Is that what you thought?'

Snap. As if she'd seen that thread break, he whirled round on her at last, his eyes burning bright and dark. 'I thought they were wrong. How could we have everything else, but be unable to have one single child? How could a woman as strong as you, as *perfect* as you, almost *die* doing what millions of women do every day?'

She frowned at the intensity with which he spoke—as if her flaw insulted him. 'Millions of women still die every year in childbirth.'

He shuddered. 'Not you, not you,' he muttered beneath his breath.

'It's a danger to all women,' she said quietly, wondering why her imperfection was such an impossibility to him. 'I got an infection when I was twelve, Jared. It happens. It could have affected my brain or heart. I could have died then. I have to live with what it did do to me.'

'Don't say it,' he snarled. 'Don't talk about it!'

'I have to. This is my reality now. *I can't have children.*'

He strode to her, grabbing her by her shoulders, eyes blazing with light. 'There's a way, Anna. It's not impossible. We can—'

Unable to bear hearing what she knew he had planned, she had to deflect him. 'There is no "we".' She shook him off, gently but with finality. 'You can't keep living the dream for us both, Jared. I don't want to live it any more.'

'You gave me your word—whatever I want,' he growled, low and intense.

She forced a shrug. 'If I have Melanie, if Rosie wants us to adopt her, I'll stay—but I won't want to be here. I won't want to be your wife, and I don't want to live here any more.'

'I refuse to believe it,' he grated out. 'It's always been us, Anna. It'll always be you and me, here at Jarndirri.'

'No.' Aching, she stepped back. 'There's no "us" now—and there never will be while your heart and soul is on Jarndirri.'

Now he frowned. 'Why not?'

She tried to think of something to say to convince him—he wouldn't listen to the truth— but eventually she shrugged and said, 'I lost my mother here, when I was only four. My grandpa Curran died here a year later, and my dad when I was twenty-three. I lost five babies here. Adam's body is here.' She bit her lip. 'Don't you get it, Jared? This place is my pain, my past. I need to find a future away from here. I need to find a way to be happy, and it isn't here.'

'But you know I can't just up and leave…' He closed his eyes. 'You don't just mean Jarndirri, do you? *I'm* also your pain, your past. I remind you of all you lost.'

'Yes,' she said, softly, sadly.

'And you're not willing to fight for us, to make things better, to be happy here with me.'

Oh, why did he have to make this so hard? Her eyes stung and burned. 'What is there to fight for? You've been fighting for a dream that never had substance…at least, not with me.' He wavered in her vision as tears rose unbidden. 'Let me go, Jared. Let me find the life and person I want to be. Take Jarndirri. I don't want any part of it.'

'No.' Without warning he turned on her, sneering lips, dead-white face. 'Keep your blood money. I won't assuage your guilt. This place can fall to ruin before I'll take a bloody cent from you, or a single acre of this place.'

The ball had been hit right out of the park; the arrow had hit the bull's-eye. She'd wanted him to take the place and continue her father's dreams, so she could leave without regret.

Without guilt.

She flushed and wheeled away. 'Then we'll sell it in the divorce proceedings, and take half each. It was left to us both. It should be enough for you to buy a smaller place, or bring Mundabah Flats to its former glory.'

'I'll never go back there.'

There it was again, that deep-waters-covering-murky-depths tone she'd heard so often, but she'd never connected it to any one thing before. But this was the second time he'd spoken that way about Mundabah. 'Why not?' she asked slowly, digging in what she was certain was the right hole at last.

He waved a hand in frozen dismissal. 'I'd rather work as a jackaroo on the worst drought-ridden property in the state than go back. My mother and her failure of a husband are welcome to it.'

'Why?' she pressed.

His eyes flashed. 'Don't go there, Anna.'

She laughed, half incredulous, half pitying. 'Why, what will you do to me, freeze me out again? Refuse to kiss me? I meant what I said just now. I'm going to divorce you, Jared.'

His face had stilled, like a marble carving, beautiful and cold. 'You always were a pitiful poker player, showing your hand too early. If

nothing I can do will change your mind, if I'm
losing the life I want, I have no incentive at all to
tell those little white lies to the adoption authorities, do I?'

Anna felt all the blood drain from her face.

CHAPTER SEVEN

JARED watched Anna sway in her seat, her eyes blank out with devastation, and he hated himself for the lie he'd told. But if she knew he'd go through with the adoption, she'd divorce him after she had what she wanted, and leave without a backward glance.

He slammed the emotional lid down on his conscience. This was the fight of his life. He had to be heartless, not rush to be her hero for once, or he'd lose her.

Not an option.

'Well?' He kept his tone cold, without mercy.

She didn't move for a long time. Only the slight rise and fall of her chest told him she was breathing at all. Her fingers twitched, like they always did when she was stressed.

After a long time, she nodded. 'You win... again,' she whispered. 'I'll stay.'

Tears ran down her cheeks. Her soft golden-brown skin had drained of all colour until it looked like alabaster. As her head drooped, her hair slowly fell over her face, a toffee-coloured curtain hiding her emotions from him.

Withdrawing into the world she'd wandered the past year, lonely and grieving and lost. She looked exactly as she had the day Adam had died, and he'd sent her back there so he could win, so he could have what he wanted. *At Anna's expense...*

'God help me, what have I done?' he muttered beneath his breath.

Every part of him ached to take her in his arms, say he didn't mean it, that she could have the blasted baby or anything else she wanted—but when he took a step, she rose to her feet. Head still lowered, she lifted a hand. 'You can force me to stay with you, but you can't make me want to be here. You can force me to be your wife, but you can't make me love you.'

The half-whispered words froze him where he stood. The one thing he'd gambled on this whole time was that she loved him still, that all these months of denial was grief talking...but somehow, now, he *felt* it.

It was over. She didn't love him. She didn't want to stay.

Stooping down to gather Melanie into her arms, she walked out of the room with an unsteady step—but at the door, she paused.

'I don't understand,' she whispered through a throat so thick he barely heard her. 'Everything I ever did was for you, in an effort to make you happy. I even left so you could have Jarndirri, and find a real woman, someone to have sons with. I gave you your dream and freedom. Why can't you let me go, Jared? Why can't you let me be happy without you?'

Until now he'd never have believed there was worse suffering than losing his son, but she'd just taken his heart from his chest while it was still beating, and walked right over it. After what seemed like hours, she still stood there, demanding answers in her silence, and he finally answered. 'It's always been you and me at Jarndirri. We belong here, together, for life. You're my *wife*.'

She looked up then—but her beautiful dove's eyes burned with fury and betrayal. 'The one thing I'd held to all these years was that you never meant to hurt me. You have no idea what you just said, do you?' She laughed, but it was an ugly sound, sad and bitter.

Moments later he heard the key turn in the lock of the room she shared with the baby.

Jared stood in the middle of the kitchen, feeling like the world's biggest fool. After all the hard work he'd done to bring her closer, he'd just pushed her away and he didn't even know why.

She was in his life, but it was the last place she wanted to be.

Why? If only he could understand what he'd said or done! He loved Jarndirri with a dreamer's passion, sure, but everything he'd done had been for them, for the family they could still have, if only she'd listen…

You can't make me love you.

At least he hadn't said the three fatal words. How many times had he heard his father say them to make his mother stay in an unendurable situation, or to ask her to fix what he'd broken? *I love you, Pauline, please make this right, make us all happy again.*

He thanked heaven he hadn't repeated history, trying to fix the unfixable with three words. If he had, Anna would only despise him for it, and rightly so.

With all his being he burned to go to her now. With a word he could make her open the door, come back to eat the forgotten lunch, or touch him—he had the power over her, until Melanie was adopted at least—but she was right. He couldn't make her *want* to be here.

He couldn't force her to love him. What was her staying worth without that?

The phone began ringing at that moment, and he knew it was Lea; it was only a matter of time before Lea called looking for Anna, especially as Anna's cellphone was switched off. 'Perfect timing,' he muttered wryly. On feet as uneven as hers had been, he crossed the room to face the tiger.

In the Wet, there were no pretty blue and violet twilights, only damp, dark shadows creeping around the clouds growing deeper by the moment. Night didn't fall, it just happened. Anna waited that long to leave her room, though she was amazed Jared hadn't forced her out long before now. He'd proven his ownership, his power over her. Was he waiting to starve her out, so she'd have to come to him like a supplicant? She was blowed if she'd go begging...

But when Melanie was no longer satisfied with the bottle of water, and began whimpering for her dinner, Anna knew she had to face him. She changed the baby again, and left the room with her head high. He might have what he wanted, but he'd never own her again.

She smelled the rich roasting cheesy smell, the garlic in the bread baking, and her stomach howled. Entering the kitchen, she saw it was empty—but there was a bowl of cereal for Melanie covered with plastic wrap, and a bottle of her favourite red wine from the Barossa Valley open and breathing.

He'd bought the wine she'd always loved?

Sounds of scraping on the front verandah led

her that way. Picking up Melanie's bowl first—it even had a little spoon in it—she walked through the screen door.

Soaking wet, Jared was scrubbing the rust off the legs of the travel cot; the inside was already clean, the thin pillows sewn together to make a mattress, a sheet over it. He looked up with a grin when she came out. 'Hey. Have a good rest?'

Anna blinked. What was he doing, acting as if nothing had happened? Opening her mouth to say *no,* she heard an uncertain 'Yes, thank you,' escape her lips.

Maybe her heart was wiser than her mind. She was tired of the arguments, of the constant struggle to win when she only ended up losing.

'That looks better,' she remarked, noting he'd done the work on the side of the house where the Buttons wouldn't see or hear him.

'I couldn't put Melanie in something that dirty, she could get sick.'

It was the first time he'd used Melanie's name without hesitation…and he was showing concern for the baby's welfare. Touched despite the lingering anger and humiliation roiling through her, she smiled.

Then the baby howled, and Anna sat down quickly, Melanie on her lap, and took the plastic cover from the bowl. 'Thanks for having it ready.'

'It was the least I could do.'

She had to keep her eyes on Melanie as she fed her, but the note in his voice, curiously humble, distracted her. She didn't pretend to misunderstand. 'I don't like being blackmailed.'

'I didn't know any other way to keep you with me.'

In all the years she'd known him, she'd never heard such an open admission from the great Jared West; he'd always been so sure of himself, so strong. 'It won't work,' she said quietly, soothingly for Melanie's sake. 'It won't make you happy, Jared, if I don't want to be here.'

He left off scraping rust, and came to her. He was still soaking wet, his black hair plastered to his forehead, his eyes like the deep indigo twilight hidden by the clouds. 'Give me a chance, Anna. I want to get it right. I can't stand to think you're going to walk away from me when I know all we could have been, if only I hadn't taken you for granted.'

His honesty compelled her to be open in return. 'I never wanted your solutions, Jared. I wanted you to listen to me, to care about how I felt.'

His gaze searched her face. 'Are you so unhappy at Jarndirri, Anna—or was it me that made you unhappy?'

Having Melanie's mouth open for more food gave her a moment's respite to think. She spooned more cereal into that little rosebud mouth, with a rush of love and joy that confused her, given Jared's question and her certainty until now. 'I don't know,' she said at last.

'You said you were tired of being alone. Did I make you feel so lonely?'

Strange that, when Jared was asking her the right questions at last, when he seemed to be listening after all these years, it felt so surreal, like she was having one of those dreams so vivid and real, she almost believed it was true. She'd wanted this for so long, but now it was here, she wasn't ready to answer. 'Melanie's dribbling her food,' she said, for something to say. 'Could you get one of her bibs? I forgot.'

She waited for one of his teasing comments, such as *What would you do without me?* but he merely nodded and went inside, giving her space, time—and he took longer than he'd need to find the bib in the baby bag. When he came back out, he had a container of wet wipes as well as the bib, and a damp cloth. 'I didn't know which you'd want, so I brought them all.'

Anna felt as if the world had slowed down, turned the other way. Jared was giving her choice… 'Thanks…um, the damp cloth, I think.' She wiped down Melanie's front and her face, put the bib on and put another spoonful into her mouth when she wailed. 'You really bought a lot of things today,' she said. *Lame, Anna, so lame!*

'The wine, the wet wipes—the pillows for the travelling cot. You were really busy.'

'I wanted to make you happy.'

The simple words, filled with all the emotion she'd once have given her life to hear, somehow became the last straw on this roller-coaster of a day. 'Stop it, Jared. I'm not ready—I don't know what you want me to say. You're confusing me. All these years of no talking at all from you, and now…' She shook her head. 'I just want to feed the baby and have dinner.'

A loud grumble of her stomach came louder than the drumming rain. Jared laughed—with an effort, it seemed to her. 'Stupid male, throwing hard questions at a hungry woman and expecting answers. I'll go serve our dinner. Want to eat it here?'

'Yes, please,' she said, more confused than ever.

The lasagne was rich tomato and strong cheese, with a Parmesan and chives top—and irresistible to the baby. Melanie kept reaching for it, delighted with the cheesy texture until the heat bit into her fingers and she screamed.

'Wait,' Jared said as she used the damp cloth to cool Melanie's fingers. He ran into the driving rain, coming back two minutes later with an article of furniture she'd thought had gone to the Lowes: the wooden high chair she'd bought, but painted herself in sky blue for a boy, with a slightly crooked Donald and Daisy Duck. 'I didn't give it all away,' he said huskily, seeing her expression. 'I tried to. I couldn't stand seeing them around the house, knowing he was gone…but I couldn't make myself give it all to them. It felt too much like I was throwing Adam away.'

The simple honesty of his grief—the first time he'd said anything so true about their son— unlocked something in her soul. Tears stung her eyes, ran down her face. 'Jared…'

'But I think he'd like us to go on,' he murmured as though the words choked him, 'and for another baby to use what he couldn't, if she makes his mummy happy.'

He wiped down the high chair, and lifted Melanie into it. 'Here we go, little girl,' he crooned, and as he held her, he rubbed his nose gently into her belly. Melanie promptly forgot the remnants of her pain and chuckled. Jared blew a raspberry into her neck, and Melanie shrieked with joy, tugging his hair with tiny fists. With a low laugh that almost rang true, Jared put her in the chair, and strapped her in safely.

Needing to add to the atmosphere, Anna ran inside and grabbed two of Jared's arrowroot biscuits, came back out and handed Melanie one.

'Now we can eat,' Jared said, pouring wine into two glasses as if he hadn't just moved her to the soul with his words about Adam. *It felt too much like I was giving Adam away.*

She should always have known why he'd given

their baby things away—and she understood why he hadn't given them all away.

And just when she needed the sustaining power of her anger against Jared, it drained away.

I didn't know any other way to keep you with me.

He kept the conversation light through dinner, playing with Melanie whenever Anna lapsed into silence, trying to think her way through the confusion he'd created in her.

They bathed the baby together. Jared played with Melanie, tickling and blowing raspberries, while Anna hunted out clean pyjamas from the clean load of washing.

Jared did the dishes while Anna folded the washing and put the baby in her new cot, safe and snug. There was a curious sense of unity as they worked around each other in a way they'd never seemed to achieve before. And why that added to her nerves, she had no idea.

And the clock ticked towards the time when she'd have to answer his questions, a slow, relentless march that still went too fast. He was giving her time, but it felt like there wasn't enough time in the world for her to know what to say.

Then Melanie fell asleep over her night bottle, exhausted because she hadn't had much of an afternoon nap, and the clock stopped. The pulsing beat of rain stopped. A hush fell over Jarndirri, as if the world waited for what she had to say.

And there was nothing. Her mind was blank.

'Let's go back to the verandah,' Jared said quietly when she came into the kitchen, wishing she was anywhere but there. He put out a hand, and after a moment punctuated by a far-off rumble of thunder, a distant fork of lightning, even knowing what would come if she touched him, she still put her hand in his.

As they passed through the wide screen door, he flicked a switch on the remote control he held, and soft music filtered through the windows and open door. 'Dance with me?'

Anna felt her head lift; she stared at him for a moment, almost wonderingly. Her favourite song—'Stand By Me', from the *Urban Cowboy* soundtrack…

'Has it been that long since we danced?' he asked, with a little, wry smile as he drew her into his arms.

She felt her shoulders rise and fall, even as he moved her, slow and tender, around the damp, covered space of raw wooden flooring between the dining set and the painted wooden rails. 'Apart from obligatory dances at weddings and rodeos, I don't think we've danced since our wedding. And this song—I didn't think you'd remember…'

'We danced to this song the night we became engaged. You whispered to me that it was our song.' His mouth twitched. 'You really don't think much of me any more, to think I could forget that.'

Her lips pressed tight for a moment, controlling the emotions he so hated. 'I always knew why you married me, Jared. I had no right to expect romance, or for you to dance with me, or remember my favourite song.'

His eyes haunted, he said in her ear, 'You had every right, Anna. If I'd thought you wanted it from me, you'd have had it all along.'

Through a tight throat, she whispered, 'It's useless if I have to ask.'

Slowly he nodded. 'It's about as useless as me asking you to come back, or expecting you to stay.'

It's so strange—I'm in his arms, dancing to a song that means everything to me, our marriage and love, and I feel like a stranger, as if I don't belong...

And yet, for the first time, he seemed to understand how she was feeling without jumping in with a solution, a direction. Maybe he finally understood that there wasn't one. Accepting it was over—and yet here they were.

'Blackmailing isn't asking,' was all she said as they moved in tiny circles, almost not moving. Aching so much with love and loss, in his arms, yet seeing only an ending and no real beginning. Was there a life without Jared? He'd been her love since her first memory of him, thinking *He's so dusty for a prince.*

Soft and slow, he twirled her out, and in,

bringing her to his chest, his heart. 'I've never known any other way but to win, Anna. I fight to keep what's mine.' He put a finger to her mouth when she began to speak. 'But I don't want to win this way. You'll stay, but hate me.'

Her throat a ball of pain now, she managed to whisper, 'I couldn't hate you, Jared.'

'Do you hate Jarndirri?'

Anna sighed and shook her head.

'Then what?' he murmured in her ear, making her shiver.

'It…haunts me,' she whispered, shivering again. 'I feel bound by my father's legacy, by what you want from me. But everywhere I go, I see where my parents have been, where they lived and loved and died, where Adam could have been…the happy places where all those babies should be.' She choked as she went on. 'The ghosts of those I love walk with me, but I can't see them, I can't touch them. I feel so cold here, never knowing what could have been, and I'm so alone with the pain.'

'You couldn't talk to me?' The rough mutter resonated through her hurting heart, an echo of her endless loss.

She couldn't look at him as she parroted, with sad irony, '"*Don't go there, Anna*"'. You never wanted to know—and it doesn't matter how hard you try, you'll never understand how I feel. None of you can understand.'

'Because we can still have children.' It wasn't a question.

A tiny sigh, a nod, and she waited for it, the cutting off.

'I can't change that. Even if I had a vasectomy it's not the same thing, is it? Because then I'm giving it away. I can never know what it's like.'

The truth in his words surprised her into saying, 'I know.'

'What will leaving me achieve, Anna?' he asked quietly, holding her against his heart, as if imprinting her there.

She squeezed her eyes shut, wishing he wouldn't make this so hard. 'I barely have a memory without you in it. Every time I hurt, every time I cried, you were there.' *Breathe in, breathe out.* 'I want to be happy—I want to forget it, all of it.'

'You won't forget.' Stark words. 'You'll spend your life running from everything you see, from everything you don't see, and it's still there.'

'Is it?' Without warning the fury was back. Wrenching her hands from his, she pushed against his chest to get away. 'I wouldn't know, would I? Because you never tell me what's haunting you. In all these years, you've never once let me in, Jared. It's always "*Don't go there!*"' With a shove, she loosened his hold but didn't break it; he refused to let her go. She turned her face and said, huskily, 'I went into the marriage knowing you didn't love me, but the day before I left, Lea told me I should talk to you—that you knew about loss because you found your father the day he died…'

Jared dropped his hands from her as if she burned him. 'She told you about my father?' Hard words, cutting her like a knife. One step back, two—and the abyss between them widened as he removed his heart from her, just as he always had.

'She assumed I knew—that of course you'd tell your wife.' She lifted her chin, reliving that humiliation to keep her strong, and not cave in under the threat of his rejection. 'The day I left I asked you about your father's death, and you pushed me away. "*Don't go there, Anna.*"'

His voice sounded like metal scraping over rock, raw and burning-hot, but he didn't acknowledge what she'd said, or the depths of her betrayal. 'I never thought she'd tell you, break my confidence.'

He'd told her sister his darkest secret, but not her. It was a betrayal as strong as infidelity, and he didn't even know it. She looked up, feeling dead inside. 'You'd have married her if she'd wanted you, wouldn't you? You love her, you really do. There's a connection, an ability to talk that you and I have never had.' Suddenly, realising she was free of his hold, she turned—but there was nowhere to go, nowhere to hide. Pelting rain only slowed her down, and separated her from Melanie; he could follow her no matter where she went. She sat down on the top step, feeling the rain cool her heated feet. 'The water will cover the bottom step soon,' she murmured, feeling the inconsequentiality of it.

'I never wanted her either.'

They came from close behind her, the words she'd waited so many years to hear—but now it was a case of too little reassurance, and far too late. She sighed. 'But you love her. You really do. You might want me in your bed, but it's Lea you care about. She's the one you've always talked to.' She wiggled her bare toes in the rain. A reminder that she was alive.

He sat down beside her, pulling off his shoes and socks. 'These days I barely talk to her. She called this afternoon, but she was looking for you.'

You don't talk to me at all. Then, tired of thinking and not saying, she said it aloud. 'That might make a difference, if you ever talked to me at all.'

As if he knew she didn't want to be touched, he remained those few inches away—but she felt something in him straining, trying to get close, to see inside her. 'I've been the one talking the past few days.'

'No,' she said quietly, 'you haven't said one

single thing that tells me about you. You've done everything in an effort to get me to talk. You don't tell me anything unless it has the ultimate purpose of making me feel, making me speak. Keeping The Curran on Jarndirri. Do you think I'm blind?' Small tears slipped from her eyes. 'Even the high chair—our son's chair—you used it, and your feelings, to make me open to you, so I'd connect to you, and stay. But you won't open to me. You never have.' When he didn't answer after five seconds, she dipped her feet in a little puddle in the dip in the old bottom stair; when he didn't speak in thirty seconds, in a minute, she stood. 'I'm going to bed now.'

Jared jerked to his feet then, and twisted her round to face him. 'What do you want from me, Anna?'

Expecting life and fire and command, all she saw in his eyes was hopeless confusion. Something in her cried out, wanting to help; but she had nothing to give. 'I've told you what I want. Melanie, and no more. Goodnight.'

'No. That's not all you want. I know it, can feel it.' He was in front of her before she could make the door and safety. In his eyes, his whole face, was a desperate kind of resolution. 'For years I knew when you had something hard to say—and whenever I didn't want to hear it or deal with your feelings, I told you not to go there. Now I'm seeing it, and I'm saying it. Do it, Anna. Go there.'

His body quivered like a bowstring pulled tight, unleashing what had always been held back before—but now it was she that felt the confusion. 'Why?' She spread her arms wide. 'Why now, Jared, when it's too late, when it can't matter?'

'It isn't too late, Anna.' He grabbed her by the shoulders, alive, vivid and blazing with all the emotion she'd wanted to see for so long. 'And it matters to me.'

'Why didn't you want to know when it mattered to *me*?' she whispered. 'Why did you always push me away when it mattered to *me*?'

The life and eagerness dimmed; he frowned, and slowly shook his head. 'I don't know. I wish to God I knew, but I don't. I thought we had it all. I couldn't see what you could lack in our life, when I was so happy with what we had.' Low, he added, 'I didn't want to know. I didn't want to change anything for you.'

She'd always known that. Her head fell, and she stood before him, like a candle snuffed as she told the truth. 'Love, Jared. I lacked love. Sex and Jarndirri was never enough for me. I wanted talk and cuddles, laughter and jokes and a friend, not just a lover. I don't want a man who takes me or my love for granted. I wanted—no, I *want*—someone who cares about how I feel *before* I walk out.'

His hands fell from her, ripping through his

hair. 'God help me—I didn't know, Anna. I could promise to change, but I don't think I can—'

'I know you can't.' She nodded with infinite sadness. 'That's what hurt the most. You see Lea—you always saw her, cared for her, went out of your way for her—but you were blind to me apart from your own needs. You didn't see me until I was gone.'

'No,' he corrected her, his voice dead. 'I saw you when you collapsed. I saw you every moment on the operating table. I saw you when the doctor told you about the hysterectomy. I've seen you every day, every hour since. Even when you weren't here, I saw you.'

'And still you said "*Don't go there*". You still didn't want to know how I felt, the day after I almost died,' she retorted, gentle and remorseless.

In the dim light hanging from the eaves, she saw him pale. 'Yes.' A hand passed over his brow. 'I did say it. I closed off. And I've regretted it every day since. For what it's worth, Anna, I'm sorry, so damned sorry I shut you out.'

Her chin lifted. 'Prove it. Tell me about your father's death, how you found him. Tell me why your father haunts you.'

He jerked back so fast he staggered into the screen door. He didn't have to say *no*. Every line of his body said it for him.

She nodded again. 'I didn't think so.' With careful deliberation she turned and walked around the side of the house, to where wide French doors opened from the room she shared with Melanie, opened them and walked in, locking herself in on both sides.

She lay dry-eyed through the night, hearing all the ringing death knells of her marriage she'd missed, so young, so in love—so blind and wilfully stupid. Missing every sign, she saw them now—but what she couldn't see was any way to fix them.

And in the warm, wet half-darkness of the deserted verandah, Jared finished the sentence she'd interrupted. 'I don't think I can ever tell you in words how much you mean to me.'

Then he turned and walked into the driving rain. *The animals, practise the words again on the animals. I love you, Anna...*

CHAPTER EIGHT

SOME time before dawn, grizzling screams made Jared jerk awake in his bed. Melanie sounded distressed. He pulled on the pyjama pants he hadn't bothered with before, and moved to the room Anna shared with the baby. A crack of brightness beneath the door showed the light was on.

He waited a few moments to see if Anna could get the baby under control, but when the crying grew more indignant, he opened the door very quietly.

Anna was holding the baby over her shoulder, rocking her back and forth, patting her downy little head and whispering, 'Come on, sweetheart, sleep time, it's sleep time…' Two empty bottles and a wet disposable nappy lay on Anna's bed. Anna was pale, with black rings beneath bleary eyes, and a deeper distress coming from her failure as Melanie screamed afresh.

She must be exhausted, he thought with a shot of tenderness and self-recrimination. Had the baby cried earlier, tonight or the night before, and he'd missed it?

'Give her to me,' he said softly, so he didn't startle her.

Anna blinked and stared at him, blinking over and over. 'What?'

Compassion filled him. Exhaustion was written over her face like an unspoken poem. 'How long has she been crying?'

She frowned, patting the baby's bottom through the nappy. 'I don't know. What time is it now?'

He checked his watch. 'Nearly five.'

She sighed and patted Melanie again as she wailed. 'Oh. Um. About three or four hours. I think it's her teeth, but there's no paracetamol or anything for her in the baby bag Rosie gave me.' She swayed on her feet.

'You need to sleep,' he said gruffly. 'Give her to me.'

He saw the torn look in her eyes—did she admit failure for the need of sleep? Then her expression became one of pure longing. She needed sleep that badly.

He felt the storm of anguish, loss and fear of losing her again, raging in him for two days, quiet and still as he waited. Anna needed him now, but she needed to recognise it herself.

'Has Melanie been waking every night?' When she hesitated and nodded, he chided gently, 'You should have called me.' He'd always managed on four to five hours' sleep a night. Anna had never coped without a full eight hours.

He saw it again, the longing for rest, the fear of failure. 'It's not your problem…'

About to take the baby from her anyway—Anna was swaying on her feet—he saw the word *mistake* flashing at him in neon letters, and he kept his distance. 'If Rosie goes through with the adoption, the adoption people will need to see I'm comfortable with her, and vice versa. That's not going to happen if you do everything—and they won't think much of us as a family for her if you're falling down with tiredness. Let me help you, Anna. Please,' he added, with the melting tenderness filling him.

She blinked again and shook her head, as if doubting her ears. Had it been so long since he'd asked anything of her, let alone said 'please'? He couldn't remember.

Then she nodded, handing the baby to him. 'Thank you. She's had two bottles already, and she has a clean nappy,' she whispered, falling asleep standing up. 'Wake me in an hour…'

With a hand at her back he turned her around, and helped her onto the bed. She was asleep before she hit the pillow.

Then he realised the wails had stopped. He looked at Melanie, and saw the flushed face wet from crying, the star-blue eyes looking at him in pleading and trust. *Help me.*

Resent her as he had for taking Anna's focus from their marriage, taking her love from him, never in his life had Jared been able to resist a cry for help. Anna deserved the rest, and Melanie was so little, so helpless...

He gathered her up, grabbed a clean bottle, a spare nappy and cleaning stuff from the bag, and slipped back outside the door, closing it behind him. He carried her through to the kitchen, and automatically filled the kettle with water for a bottle—and a coffee. 'Now what's wrong, little one?' he asked softly as he jiggled her on his shoulder.

As if in answer, Melanie began crying again, pulling on her ears in obvious pain...and it came to him, a memory floating up from nowhere. 'Are those nasty teeth bothering you?' he crooned, trying to think. His mother had always given the kids baby paracetamol or some herbal drops. He didn't have either here, and Anna said there were none in the bag. If he didn't stop her crying soon Anna would wake up and try to take over.

He handed the baby a teething rusk, but knew that, though she gurgled happily as she bit down hard with her gums, it was only a temporary measure. She needed pain relief to return to sleep. He changed her nappy again and put her pyjamas back on, knowing he was running out of time.

He needed expert help here, and there was only one person he knew who had both the knowledge of babies and could be trusted to keep their secret, no matter what. He picked up the phone and dialled Lea's number.

Within moment's Lea's voice, rough and growly with sleep, answered. 'This had better be good, West.'

She'd obviously checked caller ID—and Lea always called him West when she was in a mood. He grinned, liking it as usual, but got to the point. 'I need to know, without questions asked, what I can use to stop a baby's teething pain. I don't have paracetamol for babies or the herbal drops Mum used. Anything I can use that's in the cupboard?'

'*A baby?*' Lea wasn't asking, she was demanding to know—same old Lea.

'I don't have time now, Lea. If I don't help her soon, she'll start crying and wake Anna, and she hasn't slept properly in days.'

'*Anna?* She's back with you?'

Melanie was beginning to grumble. Jared gave an exaggerated sigh. 'Can we do this at some decent hour, Lea? I'll call you some time tomorrow and give you the story. Right now I have a crying baby, and I need my question answered. The poor kid's in pain here.'

'She needs chamomile,' she answered promptly,

having picked up on the one 'she' he'd used re-garding Melanie. 'Use tea bags if you don't have drops. Add a touch of honey—just a bit—or she'll spit it back out. It doesn't taste the best.'

'Drops?' he asked, feeling stupid—then a thought occurred to him. If Anna hadn't known what they were for… He put Melanie down and ran back to the room, grabbed the baby bag and ran out before he could disturb Anna. 'What would they look like?' he asked, rummaging in the bag while Melanie screamed louder.

'Boy, she really needs help.' Lea's voice was filled with sympathy for the baby's pain. 'They're usually in a little dark bottle with a squeeze-top dropper. You put a few drops in watered-down juice—the water has to be boiled first.'

'Uh-huh,' he mumbled as he started tossing out stuff that wasn't what he needed; he knew the water needed boiling. In a little, sealed separate bag, he found a small dark bottle, and held it up to read—'Thank heaven,' he muttered, 'I've got the chamomile drops. Can I add it to the formula?' he asked, wondering if they had any tetra bricks of juice left. The nearest store was two hours' flight away, and juice wasn't his thing. He drank coffee and beer.

'Ick, no! Would you drink chamomile tea with milk?'

He chuckled in half-relief as he found a tetra

brick of 100 per cent apple juice, and ripped it open. 'I wouldn't drink that stuff at all.'

'Oh, sure, you're a real Outback man, beer and meat only. You don't eat quiche or drink herbal teas,' she mocked, laughing now. 'Just get the juice and water ready with the drops, and make it gently warm so she can drink it right away. But this takes quite a bit longer to work than medication, so soak a rusk in the juice and drops—she can chew on it and get faster relief.'

'Thanks, mate,' he said softly, with a rush of affection, putting the phone on speaker so he could pick up Melanie, who was at ear-splitting level now, and make the bottle at the same time.

'Yeah, whatever. I'll send you a baby rescue package by priority—email me a list of what you need, and I probably have it somewhere from when Molly needed it. But I want that call tomorrow, West—today, in fact. I want *details*. And I want to talk to Anna.'

'Yeah, yeah.' He chuckled, putting the juice into the bottle with half water. He hesitated for a moment before he said, 'Lea—about the baby…'

'I get it, Jared,' she said quietly, without the acerbity that was so much a part of her nature. 'I don't know whose kid she is, but I know you—and I know my sister. Anna will tell me when she's ready. I'll keep the secret. But this had better not be illegal, or some trick. Anna deserves better than that.'

Lea was blunt, but could give great hints when she chose. Anna deserved better than he'd been giving her in years. He got it. 'It isn't either one, and I knew you'd keep it to yourself.'

'Yeah, whatever, West. Just fix the baby, get some sleep, and call me today. Look after my baby sister.' The *click* of disconnection followed.

Melanie fought against drinking the juice at first, pulling faces and spitting it out. Jared firmly kept putting the teat back in her mouth. 'Come on, little one, work with me here,' he crooned as she still resisted, wanting the milk she was used to. His scrambled brain went into overdrive as he tried to find a way to distract her. He hid behind the bottle for a second, popped around it with a crazy face and said, softly, 'Boo.'

Melanie gurgled, and swallowed a mouthful of the drink.

He played the game over and over with her, making a different face every time for her, and she drank in response. When the bottle was empty, she still wasn't sleepy, so he handed her the soaked rusk to chew. Melanie shoved it in her mouth, but looked at him with an expectant *what game do we play now* look in her bright eyes. Though he'd done little to deserve it, Melanie liked him—and she trusted him without words to make her happy.

He only wished Anna could do the same beyond tonight—or that he knew what would make her happy, so she'd want to stay.

Jared scrubbed at his own weary eyes, and thought. 'You're a girl, and your new mummy seems to like dancing…maybe it's a girl-thing. Okay, little one, how about we dance you to sleep?' He walked her into the living room, found the CD remote and clicked on the player.

It was an album of Anna's she hadn't taken, a compilation she'd made of her favourite songs from CDs she'd bought. He didn't particularly like them—or thought he hadn't—but he found, as he waltzed the baby slowly around the room, he knew every word of the songs. He sang 'Ain't No Sunshine', 'True Colours' and others without even thinking about it. His voice was rough, but Melanie didn't seem to mind. She tweaked his nose, pulled his ear and his hair, and giggled with the delicious, rich joy in living only children have the secret of knowing, and adults wished they could find again. 'It's true,' he assured a slightly sleepy baby during the melody. 'This house isn't a home without her.'

Then Melanie fell forward in the movement of the dance, and wet, rusk-covered lips brushed his cheek by accident. A slushy baby-kiss touched with magic… Moved, he looked at Melanie, and couldn't take his gaze from her. Dancing around the room, singing to a kid he'd only tolerated until now, or pretended to like to make Anna happy, the tough Outback man was lost in a baby's eyes, fixated on a drooling smile...

And suddenly he knew: in one of those flashes of truth that came rarely in life, Jared knew. He saw in a silly midnight dance and baby-kiss all the mistakes he'd made with Anna—and he knew what to do. He only prayed to God he wasn't too late.

'Let's walk on some sunshine, little one,' he murmured as the song began.

From behind the half-closed door of the living room, Anna, who kept waking up anxious, wondering how Jared was coping, hearing the gravelly voice singing and the baby giggles, watched as a man who'd always seemed as cold and remote as the stars melted for a tiny girl that wasn't his. And even as she smiled, she ached for what could have been. If only he could have been this man for *her*.

Then she heard the words he'd never have said if he'd known she was there: *This house isn't a home without her.* And deep inside her, something she'd thought was shut down for ever clicked softly back to *on*.

She turned and crept quietly back to her bed. Melanie was safe and happy, in strong, trustworthy arms. And she, Anna, needed a safe place to let her heart overflow.

* * *

He was gone again the next morning when Anna woke, but had left the breakfast for Melanie and coffee for her. He'd even made a breakfast muffin for her, with bacon and eggs kept warm.

There was a note on the bench.

Back soon. We still have the stables to muck out. ☺

Strangely, Anna found herself smiling and singing to herself—the songs he'd sung to Melanie last night—as she fed the baby.

She found delight even in Melanie spitting the food at her, because the baby shrieked in happiness at the mess she'd created. Tiny fingers wiped the mush into Anna's face and hair, and Anna just sat there laughing, touching that sweet, flushed little face, petting the spiky hair, all damp from the extreme humidity outside, as well as in.

Within days Adam and Melanie seemed to be merging into one face, a single entity of adorable baby, and she loved them both. Motherhood, to have a baby to love, was worth any sacrifice. *Any* sacrifice.

Jared walked in two hours later, as Anna finished cleaning the house with the baby crawling around after her, making a mess of what she'd cleaned. He lifted his brows, pointing. 'Has Melanie begun crawling? She's pretty young for that.'

Even looking at him reminded her of the man she'd seen last night, so moved by a baby-kiss. Aching with wistfulness, longing and regret, Anna made herself laugh. 'Yes. I sat her down on the floor with some toys so I could sweep—she doesn't seem to like the portable cot when she's awake—and the second she saw the dust and dirt, she got down on hands and knees and came after me.' Awe and joy swept through her, thinking of it: she'd seen a milestone in Melanie's life…her first crawling step…

He grinned. 'Has she been crawling behind you, making mess, all morning?'

She chuckled. 'The things they don't tell you about the joys of parenthood.'

'So it seems.' Eyes shimmering with humour met hers. 'So do we dare take her out to the stables without the cot?'

This time she burst out laughing, and snorted. 'Oh, the fun she'd have with the animals—and the dung!'

'Yeah,' he said softly. 'I remember the best times of my childhood were chucking the stuff around—especially at my sisters and brothers—and Mum running around with a wooden spoon, trying to catch me, for all the work I caused.' He chuckled. 'She never did catch me. She always said I drove her up the wall, so I'd make car engine sounds and run to walls.'

He was talking about his family life again, and it felt as if she couldn't stop smiling, laughing—and that felt so good. For the longest time she'd wondered if she'd forgotten how to laugh spontaneously. 'I see my future before me. Melanie already painted my face with her breakfast. If Rosie does let us adopt her, I somehow don't think I'll be getting the decorous little girl I was.'

'Except when you stole chocolate,' he reminded her, his eyes still laughing, not sensual—but still she caught her breath for a moment.

She lifted a shoulder. 'A pathetic kind of rebellion, wasn't it?' she asked lightly. 'During her lifetime, the rebel Lea runs away from boarding school, refuses to marry the man her father picks for her, starts her own place and makes a total success of it, has a child and won't marry the father. And what do I do in my entire life? I steal chocolate—once.'

'I thought it was adorable,' he said quietly.

That was the problem. You saw me as a child to protect and adore, not a woman to love. She turned to sweep up the mess Melanie was happily grubbing around in. 'Can you grab her and distract her with something?'

'I bought her some toys this morning. Don't worry, I said they were for Molly's next visit,' he added when she whirled back on him in panic. 'Come on, little darlin', let's get you playing with the good stuff.'

Unfortunately for them, Melanie's idea of *the good stuff* was the dust bunnies Anna had swept, lifting them in her hands and letting them float to the ground. She started screaming the second he put her in the chair, and threw the toys away in disgust, even pushing at Jared when he tried to distract her by making faces.

Jared shrugged and put her back in the mess. 'The house can stay dirty for now. We need to keep her quiet another day or two. Any more than that and the Wet's too set in to get here easily. Any sooner and it looks suspicious.'

'I know.' That had been her plan. Trying not to feel annoyed that, as usual, he was taking control of a situation that was *hers*, Anna watched the baby gurgle happily as the unsettled dust bunnies floated around her face. She felt her entire being melt with love. 'She likes to see things moving.'

'Then she'll love the stables and the animals.' He was watching Melanie, his gaze guarded yet softer than anything she'd seen from him.

Keep accord with him, keep your cool. But the memory of him dancing with Melanie last night still haunted her—the look in his eyes, like an iceberg hitting the equator at warp speed, melting...

She was glad they'd bonded, but she couldn't

help wondering, *Why didn't he ever melt for me? Why could he think me adorable but never love me?*

This house isn't a home without her, he'd said so softly…and the confusion filled her again.

'When do you want to go out to the stables?' she asked, hanging on to her equanimity with everything she had.

He was on his haunches now, tossing the dust balls in the air, grinning as the baby shrieked with laughter. 'Hmm… What did you say? After her nap is fine.' He tossed another dust bunny for Melanie. 'Want me to give her a bottle and change her for bed while you make lunch?'

It was a fair offer, since he'd been cooking or bringing home meals so much, yet, watching him smiling so—so infatuatedly as Melanie tossed dirt at him and he laughed, Anna felt only resentment, anger, pain—loss. *She's mine, stop taking everything away from me!*

When we leave here, she'll forget him soon enough, and he'll have his own children. Sooner or later.

'Sure.' Walking on legs that shook only a little, she crossed to the fridge to pull out a salad, and a bottle to heat in boiled water. 'I'll check on the animals while you get her settled,' she said, feeling as brittle as broken glass.

'Anna?'

The unspoken question—the new uncertainty

in a voice always filled with authority—made her gulp; his closeness intensified her shivers. 'I'm fine. Just get her settled.'

'I'll make lunch. You fix her up,' he said, too quiet. He knew, and wanted to fix it.

She shook her head. 'Go ahead. As you said last night, the adoption people will need to see us both bonded to her—and her to us.'

She heard the frown in his voice, the confusion. 'You sound angry. I thought you wanted me to bond with her.'

If only it was anger! But it wasn't. The jealousy was eating at her—yes, for Melanie's love, but stronger was the useless wishing for what she'd never had from him, the regret for what never came—the love he'd given to a stranger's baby so quickly.

She couldn't look at him as she faced the truth: she could run to the ends of the earth and she'd never forget him, never truly get over him or have a complete heart. It would always be here…at Jarndirri. With Jared.

The worst part was, she knew she could have him. All she had to do was say she'd changed her mind, she wanted to stay—and she'd have the rest of her life with him. Having what she'd signed on for when she'd married him—working the land together, living out their lives together, in bed, at Jarndirri, in their community.

Watching him love Melanie more day by day as she grew, aching for the love he'd never have to give her. Would she end up resenting her baby for being more lovable than she was?

'I do want you to bond with her.' Was that her voice, so gentle, so polite, when she felt like screaming, *Go away and leave us alone*? She grabbed the bottle out of the jug of hot water, shook it and put it into his hand. 'Go put her to bed. I'm fine.'

Hands lifted her hair; warm lips brushed the back of her neck, and she shivered with its power, the hopeless longing that would never change. 'I'll be back in ten minutes.'

Unable to speak, she nodded. The more time the better. She needed to find distance from him somehow.

CHAPTER NINE

WITHIN five minutes he was in the room once more, but no matter how hard she'd tried to think of what to say, she wasn't ready for the look in his eyes. 'I'm not hungry,' he said quietly, when she put two plates of salad, condiments and some sliced bread on the table.

'I don't want to talk.' Desperation laced every word. She was too close, too raw.

'I know,' he surprised her by saying. There was no laughter in his voice, just a curious note she couldn't identify. 'Come here to me.'

Caught out, Anna looked at him, saw his arms held out, something like tenderness in his face. 'Don't patronise me, Jared,' she snapped, brittle, needing. 'I'm not Melanie.'

'I know,' he said again. 'But I still think you need a cuddle.'

She heard the echo of her words the night before, and something died in her. 'I told you, if

I have to say it, if I have to tell you what I want or need, it's meaningless.'

'It's not meaningless to me, Anna—and I don't believe it's meaningless to you either. Give me a chance. I want to give you what you need.'

Torn between loss and longing, she saw the look on his face once again—strong, carved from the land he loved, but no longer so remote—and her feet obeyed her craving heart. One step, another…

'I need a cuddle, too. You have no idea how much I've missed those cuddles you used to give me,' he said quietly, and he took a step toward her, and another.

'I didn't think you cared about them one way or another,' she whispered. He was coming to her, at last he was meeting her halfway, and he couldn't know what that meant to her. 'You always seemed to just put up with me needing to hold you.'

'I cared.' His eyes were dark pools of need, his voice rough, hot gravel, the land before storm. 'I…still care, Anna. I should have told you, shown you.' His eyes slowly closed as his hand reached out for hers. 'I'm so cold without you. I've been like a block of ice since you've been gone, unable to laugh or feel. I need you, Anna. Touch me. Make it right again.'

He needs me.

One more step, and she was in his arms, hers

around his waist, hearing his heart beating beneath her ear. He buried his face in her hair, breathing her in. Her eyes fluttered shut as tiny shivers filled her, warm and beautiful. And when he kissed her with a sweet tenderness she hadn't had from him since their engagement night, loneliness, so long her constant companion, melted into the furthest shadows of her mind.

He lifted her in his arms; but to her surprise he didn't carry her to the bedroom. On the fat old sofa in the living room, with the rain pounding down, he sat with her on his lap, still kissing her without demand, only with sweet caring, and a blanket of warmth surrounded her, protecting her from all the pain.

She wanted to lay her head on his shoulder; she wanted him to kiss her for ever. She wanted this man, this Jared, to be hers, forever.

'I brought something home for you,' he mumbled between kisses. His hands held her close, tiny caresses from his fingers making her feel safe and cherished.

At that, she pulled back, her gaze searching his, so uncertain. 'What are you doing, Jared? With me, I mean. All the gifts, the dancing, the kisses and cuddles—why?'

'Why not?' he murmured, and kissed her again.

'I'm serious, Jared. What are you doing?' she whispered.

His expression, teasing and sweet only seconds before, sobered. The words came, slow and unsure. 'I'm courting my wife.'

The four words took her breath away. 'Why?'

He frowned, struggled with the answer. 'I'm giving you the romance I never gave you from the night I put that ring on your finger.'

Anna was trembling in his arms, wanting to bolt, needing to stay, to hear it. 'Why?'

'Because you deserve it—you always did.' He shrugged and added with devastating candour, 'I took everything you wanted to give, and what you didn't want to give. I pushed you into my life and dreams, and never once questioned whether you shared them…not even when you left.'

She bit her lip, turned her face a little. 'It's not all your fault. I knew the deal.'

'No, you don't.'

Startled, she twisted back to him, her mouth open.

'You don't know the deal. You never did.' Eyes filled with resolution stared into hers. 'I didn't take you to have Jarndirri. That was Bryce's deal, not mine. I told him I'd only take on Jarndirri if I could have you. I said I was going to have you anyway, that he couldn't stop me, but I'd have Jarndirri as well if it was on offer.'

Anna blinked, gaping at him. 'W-what?'

He shrugged again. 'You never suspected the truth? Bryce had far grander plans for you than to marry a humble West. I was intended for Lea, to keep her here, to settle her down. He was hoping you'd marry Marcus O'Malley, to join the two properties. The Curran girls would own the biggest spread in the lower Kimberleys.'

Over two million hectares…oh, that sounded just like her driven, ambitious father. He'd always believed the small amount of fine gold her granddad had found on Jarndirri was the tip of the iceberg—that there was more on the property next door, Cormorant Station, the O'Malley home for a hundred years. To join the two would give Bryce Curran's children and grandchildren obscene wealth, and for generations to come…

And the Curran name would be remembered in history, even if the great Bryce Curran had only fathered girls.

'Why did he choose Lea for you?' she asked, frowning. It made no sense—wasn't she, Anna, the Golden Girl, most likely to—?

'You were his favourite, Anna—he wanted the best for you. Lea was getting what he figured she deserved. He also thought she'd want to keep her name when she married—and I'm guessing he knew I wouldn't care about giving up mine, and becoming a Curran.'

After a moment, she started laughing, slow and helpless. 'Oh, yes, that sounds like Dad. His middle name should have been Shylock or Machiavelli. He always did have plans to aggrandise himself, through us if he had to—and for everything he gave anyone, he wanted his pound of flesh in return.'

'Yes, he did—but he gave me a home and family, so I tried to accommodate him.'

'Of course you did. You were eighteen, nineteen, and he'd been everything to you—just as he planned to be when he took you in. Your gratitude would ensure that you did as he wanted.' Anna jumped to her feet, pacing the room. 'I'll bet he'd hand-picked you for Lea when you were kids, and Marcus for me.'

Jared frowned out the window. 'Marcus is the kind of man he wanted for you—educated at the best schools in the country, went to Oxford and did animal husbandry and law before he came back to Cormorant. He's a gentleman—and I'll always be rough around the edges.'

She had to clamp down on her mouth to stop the runaway sentence, *I like rough—I like real men*. It would only give him false hope, when she still didn't know what she wanted.

She had a sudden thought, and though she was still furious at the blatant manipulation of her life, she chuckled. 'He must've gone ballistic on you when you wanted me instead.'

Jared grinned. 'About equivalent to the force of Cyclone Tracy.'

'And you held your ground?' she asked in mock-admiration.

The grin deepened, showing reluctant dimples—the dimples he'd always hated. 'What can I say—I *really* wanted you.'

Anna bit her lip over a smile of pure pleasure. 'No way would Perfect Marcus want wild Lea! Sandra O'Malley is the model wife—just as I'd have been, if we'd liked each other as more than friends,' she added with absent bitterness.

'You were the model wife to me.'

'Yes, and look where we are now,' she retorted with more sad fatalism than anger. 'Why, Jared? Why did you rebel against Dad's plans, when it gave you everything you wanted?'

'It didn't give me everything I wanted, because I didn't want Lea. I wanted you,' he replied simply. 'It was always you.' He grinned, but it seemed to be with an effort. 'Do you remember the day we met? You probably don't—but you fell in the dirt at the rodeo, and I picked you up and dusted you off because you were wailing about the dirt on your new clothes. You were about four. I'd just turned eight. You smiled at me when I finally got you clean by dumping you in a horse trough, but I didn't get your hair or new hat wet. You asked me where my castle was. I said I didn't have one. You said all princes have castles.' He shrugged, wouldn't look at her as he said, 'I think I knew then I'd marry you.'

She bit her lip over a beatific smile. He not only remembered their first meeting, but had planned their future…

Why wouldn't he want to marry a rich girl who saw him as a prince?

Her lips pressed hard together for a moment, before she forced the words out again. The words felt like a knife twisting in her heart every time she said them. 'But you want children. You want your own kids.'

'No—I want *our* kids,' he said quietly. There was a palpable hesitation before he spoke again. 'But there are other ways to have kids, Anna—our own kids, yours and mine, if—'

'I don't want to hear it.' She wheeled hard away from him, blinking hard to push out the image of that sweet, white face, the eyes that would never open. 'I don't want alternatives or medical marvels any more. I don't want solutions to problems that are no longer mine. Again, it's your dream, Jared—*yours*. My dreams of my own children died with Adam.'

'They don't have to,' he muttered, low and hard, 'if you'd just listen—'

'No, *you* listen, Jared West. For once in your life, you are going to listen to *me*.' She turned back, hands on hips, staring him down. 'I won't go through IVF again—and I don't want to go the surrogacy route, so if you were thinking of asking

Lea or Sapphie, don't. I'd never ask another woman to bear a child only to hand it over—I've lost children, and I couldn't be so selfish as to ask others to do it when I couldn't.'

For long moments he sat frozen on the sofa. Then he covered his eyes with a hand and mumbled, 'Sapphie said she'd do it if you asked her, Anna. She said she wouldn't mind…'

Anna knew what he'd left unspoken. She and Lea had already discussed it once, watching a show on surrogacy years ago. She'd known what Lea's answer would be—she'd do it, but it would kill her sister to give away a child, just as it would kill her. 'Sapphie hasn't got a clue what you asked of her. You don't know what it's like, Jared. You never will,' she said quietly. 'You never felt your body growing, never felt the first tiny fluttering bubbles as they moved. You didn't go through the long pain of giving birth months too early, knowing they were…gone. I couldn't ask either my sister or my dearest friend to go through all the joy, all the pain of childbirth, only to hand him or her over to us.'

Anna watched in deep-hidden compassion as his dreams died before her. He sat still and white, one hand over his eyes, silent, broken.

She didn't know if this was the worst time or the only time to bring it to a finish, or twist the knife, but it had to be said. 'My dreams had been yours, Jared—and I didn't know it until you asked me to carry Adam, and didn't know or see how I felt. But no matter whose dreams they were, they died the day Adam did. If I'd had him here, I'd probably still be here, thrilled to be a mother, but part of me always unhappy, not knowing if I was living or existing as part of your world. Never knowing if you'd married me for Jarndirri, never knowing—because you would never have told me before now—if you were wishing it was Lea here instead of me.'

Slowly, during her speech, he'd looked up. Still sheet-white, eyes black with devastation, he said, 'You don't know me at all to even think that.'

'I know,' she said, her voice steady as what remained of her heart splintered. 'That was always the problem between us. I *don't* know you at all.'

'I'm trying, Anna. It might be late, but I'm trying to let you in. Wait here.' With a jerking movement, he got to his feet and walked out of the room. Within moments he was back, holding out a bag to her. 'I thought of you when I saw this.'

Confused at the change of direction when she'd been planning to end it, she found herself taking the bag, and looking inside. She felt a smile curving her mouth. 'Jared…'

'You said Jarndirri didn't feel like yours. Make

it yours—we can buy new furniture, paint the place, do whatever you want—or you take this with you when you go,' he said quietly.

Her head still spinning a little, she pulled out the three long-stitch kits—she'd always loved creating things of her own, rather than buying anything for the house—it made it her own...

And then she saw the card at the base of the bag. 'What's this?' She looked at it, and gasped. 'Oh, *Jared*...'

He was still pale, his eyes haunted—but he smiled. 'They're flying it all in this afternoon, or tomorrow morning. You always wanted to be an art teacher, but you've barely painted since your uni days. I thought you might like to take up painting again—or use your degree. The School of the Air needs teachers, and with the net and video conferencing, you could show the kids in remote areas how to make something beautiful, like that.'

He indicated the painting hanging on the living-room wall. She'd done it years ago, at boarding school: her final project she'd simply called 'Home'. Jarndirri homestead in the Wet, with jagged lightning forks crossing the sky, and men on motorbikes chasing a rogue brumby.

She looked at the order for a complete art kit: easels of varying sizes; three palettes; and paints—oils, water and acrylic; pastels; stretched

canvases and painted masonite, and felt tears
stinging at her eyes. 'I—I haven't painted
anything for years, except...' *Adam's room.*
Adam's high chair and cradle, and his hanging
toys...

She felt him pull her close. 'I know, love, I
know.' He held her against him, kissing her hair
as she wept softly, and she felt his tears wet her
hair. 'Art was your dream—and teaching kids. I
didn't think it was as important as living here,
being together, having kids. I thought what we
had, what I gave you was enough. I was wrong.'
He bent and kissed her cheek, the other. 'Have
your dreams, Anna—whether you stay or go.'

'Thank you,' she said, fumbling for words.

'Don't thank me, Anna. I'm just giving back
what you should never have lost.'

She pulled back to look at him. Yes, his eyes
were still haunted, just like her heart. So much
pain, so much past—so many loved ones lost.
Jared tangled in every memory. She could disappear, but how did she run from her life, her own
mind? How could she forget?

'I still have to go,' she said quietly, trying to turn
her face but held by the unspoken suffering in his.
He did care—care for *her*, not just Jarndirri. She
couldn't fool herself that he didn't any more.
But... 'I need to know what *I* want, Jared. I need
to find my own life.'

'And it isn't here?'

With me, he meant—but she couldn't face the question, not yet, and took him literally, because it was somehow easier. 'I don't *know*. Jarndirri's its own entity, a life force. Every part of my adult life is here—all my *life*, apart from school and uni, is here. Everything and everyone I've lost is here. It's like this huge blanket smothering me, and every breath I take hurts me.'

'Do you feel that way about me, too?'

She should have known he'd keep pushing for the answer he sought, even if it hurt them both. And it was hurting him; the tight coil of anguish inside was locked down deep, but she could see it there, ripping at him. She swallowed, breathed in and out by force. 'I don't *know*,' she cried again, feeling wretched. 'You and Jarndirri have been one entity in my mind for so long. You both dominate my life, overshadowing everything I do or I want, just as Dad and Jarndirri did. It's been that way all my life. I don't know if I can even separate you.'

His jaw moved, but nothing else. 'That's why Lea ran off to Grandad Jenkins at Yurraji,' he muttered eventually. 'The fight over marrying me was her excuse to get away from Bryce's domination—and from the obsession with Jarndirri. I always knew that.'

Anna nodded. 'She left. I had to stay…but, oh,

how I wanted to do what she's done.' *And how I admired her, and resented her, for forging her own life, her way.*

'Did you feel that way about marrying me?'

Her gaze lowered. She pressed her lips tight, chewed at her mouth. 'I was so crazy about you. You know that—I never tried to hide it. I knew you'd never be happy off the land, or with an independent wife. So I gave up what I wanted to make you happy.'

He still didn't move; she felt his stillness like a living thing. 'So you did resent me, just like you resented Lea—like you still resent her. You resent her because she got away from here—because she rebelled and didn't get punished for it. Because she has Molly, can have other kids.'

Hearing the words so bluntly stated should have shocked her, but then she realised she'd been waiting to hear them for a long time, either from him or Lea. After a few moments, she shrugged. 'And for having Molly so *casually*, a one-night stand, when we couldn't have one with all we'd tried.'

'And me?' he pressed. Pushing as usual for her emotions, so he could fix it; but this wasn't fixable, and it was time he realised that.

So she said, lightly, 'Wouldn't you have resented me, if I'd expected you to come off Jarndirri for a few years so I could teach before we settled back here to have kids?'

The frisson of surprise ran from him to her. 'I wouldn't have done it.' Low, he added, 'I never thought of giving anything up to have you.'

She nodded. 'I know.' *You just added me to your list of possessions.*

'I—cared, Anna. I still care.' He was plainly struggling to say so much.

A vast sadness rose inside her, but still she smiled. 'I know, Jared. In your way, you do care. We've known each other too long not to. But I've been lost for years, and you never even noticed when you left me behind. I don't think you wanted to see it.'

'I didn't. Then.' He strode to the window, watching the sheets of water from the heavens, like a waterfall's edge. 'There has to be a way. I'd do anything to fix this.'

'Anything but leave Jarndirri,' she said quietly.

He wheeled back round, his eyes shadowed, as if bruised. He didn't have to say it. She knew there wasn't a choice. 'I want to grow old with you, Anna. No woman but you.'

Beautiful, moving words—but he meant on Jarndirri. And he hadn't had any other woman since he'd been eighteen. He couldn't possibly mean what he'd said, even if he thought he did. 'There are women who want your dream, Jared. Women who love the land, who won't demand compromise and—and what you can't give.

Women who can have children. I'm barely a woman any more.' She almost choked on the words, they hurt so much.

'That's not true,' he murmured, eyes closed, fists clenched. 'You're my woman, the only one I want.'

Struggling against tears, she whispered, 'I can't stay here, Jared. I have to go.'

He was so still, she felt a ridiculous urge to take his pulse. Then his hand twitched; a muscle in his cheek moved, and slowly, he turned from her. 'The rain's getting worse. We'll call Rosie tomorrow at the facility, ask her if she's changed her mind. If she hasn't, we can tell the authorities about Melanie. Soon the rivers will flood, and nobody will be able to drive in. We need to get the plan into action.'

'All right,' she replied, awkward, inane. Lame, lame… 'Thank—'

'Stop.' The word was so harsh she winced. 'I've neglected your dreams, your needs for twelve years. If Melanie and your freedom is all you want from me, you'll get it.'

The words moved her to her soul. Soft, hesitant, she stammered, 'I-if I can d-do anything…'

He shook his head once. Curt, on the edge of losing control. 'You've done enough, Anna. All these years, you've done enough. Let me give to you for once.'

'Stop it. You've been the rock of this district, always giving—'

'Yes, I'm always giving, aren't I? To everyone but the one person I should have given everything to. That person I pushed into things she didn't want, and pushed her away at the same time.'

What could she say to that?

'Just know one thing.' His hands were in his pockets; his face remained resolutely watching the rain, the brilliant forks of lightning attacking the sky. 'I'll be here waiting. For the rest of my life, I'll be waiting for you to come back.'

She couldn't take any more of this. With a stifled sound, she turned and ran from the room; but the ghosts of what had been and what might have been crowded her every step—and she knew that, no matter what she did with her life, they'd always be there.

And for the rest of her life, Jared would always be there. He'd haunt every step, fill every silent moment: her personal ghost and the yardstick by which every other man would fail.

CHAPTER TEN

MELANIE awoke grumpy from her nap. Anna brought her out to the kitchen to feed her—but she threw away the bottle, dribbled over the teething rusk with a grizzling wail, turned her face from a biscuit. She even slammed her little fist in disgust over the dust bunnies Anna retrieved from the garbage.

Jared, who'd been watching, waiting for Anna to ask for help, finally gave up and said, 'I think we should distract her.'

Anna looked up at him in open pleading. 'With what?'

He grinned. 'Well, those stables are getting smellier by the hour.'

'You don't think she's too little?' She twisted her hands around each other, her gaze anxious. 'What if she eats dirt or dung—?'

'Babies in Third World countries survive worse than a bit of dirt—and as the doctor assured my mother when I apparently ate my first fistful of horse doo, it's never killed anyone yet,' he assured her in mock solemnity.

A slow smile spread across Anna's face. 'Yeah, but if you're recommending yourself as a living example of what eating poop can do to you...' She went cross-eyed and made a crazy stuttering noise, like Porky Pig's stutter, by pulling her lip down with her finger over and over.

He burst out laughing and tugged at her hair, glad she'd got past her tragic mood earlier. If he needed to inject more happy medicine into their relationship, every five minutes, he'd do it.

If only he'd thought to help her this way months ago, she might never have left.

'Come on, let's go. I've set up some blankets for her in a clean patch right near the lambs. I think she'll like them.' Though this was a cattle station, her dad had bought her a couple of sheep when she was little. Despite selling spring lambs every year, Jarndirri still had about ten dozen sheep—Anna's sheep, they were called. Her dad had even had shearers flown in every time the sheep grew too woolly, and it was accepted Jarndirri tradition now.

'No more excuses. Let's go.' He handed Anna an umbrella with which to protect Melanie both from the rain and the curious eyes of John and Ellie Button.

Melanie's bad mood broke the moment Anna

laid her on the series of blankets he'd laid out in the stable. The baby took one look at the lambs in the pen next to her, and a delicious, gurgling laugh gushed from her lips as she began crawling toward the animals.

Jared pushed a shovel into Anna's hand as she was about to run after Melanie. 'Hey, you're not getting out of the work that easily.'

'But what if she…?'

He put a finger over her lips. 'Don't you remember the fun you had in here when you were a kid? Let her go, Anna. She's happy.'

'The pen posts are rough—'

'I sanded them earlier. There's no way she'll get a splinter.' Quickly, before she could protest again, he pushed the foot-high concrete blocks he'd brought for the purpose—and nearly strained every back muscle doing it—that morning. 'There. Best playpen any kid ever had, complete with living toys to watch.'

Two hours of hard labour followed—but Anna had never minded hard work, and felt good at the end, though she was drenched in sweat and stank of dirt and dung by the time they were done. She kept running back to check on Melanie, of course, but for the most part the baby was having fun watching the lambs and hearing them bleat. She laughed every time—and she was fascinated by the horses. Whenever one whinnied she stopped whatever she was doing to fix her gaze on the beautiful creatures, with a drooling smile and incoherent baby noises of pleasure.

Anna shovelled the last load of muck into one of the massive bins kept for mulch, put the lid down tight and came back from the other end of the stable to check on Melanie. She found the baby in Jared's arms, her gold-and-silver chortles of happiness floating in the air as Jared danced her around the pen, singing loudly and off-key to her. He laughed as she tugged his hair, or put grubby fingers in his mouth, in his ear or up his nose, as babies did.

Her gaze swivelled to where the music came from. 'You brought out the portable CD player for Melanie?'

He jumped as if shot. Jared, who noticed everything, hadn't seen her there, he'd been so absorbed in the baby. 'I noticed she likes music,' he explained, gruff and cool, but Anna smiled. There was just a tinge of blush on his upper cheeks at being caught singing 'Girls Just Wanna Have Fun' to a baby.

And he'd known every word of the song. And he'd always acted as if he hated her CDs...

Grinning, she said as the music ended, 'I think it's time for a shower. I feel all sweaty—'

Realising what she'd said, and how she'd always said that before, she glanced at him in half-aroused horror, and saw in his eyes a mirror of her memory, and her desire. She burst into speech, almost babbling. 'Do you think Melanie will be okay in a shower with me? It'll be faster if we shower together—' She skidded to a horri- fied halt, shut her mouth and then babbled again, 'Melanie and me, I mean, not…' Now she closed her eyes. Could she have made it any worse? Could she be any more humiliated, any *needier*? Why didn't she just say, *Take me to bed*?

'I think she's getting tired. If you shower her quickly and hand her to me, I can give her a bottle and dress her while you dress, and we can put her to bed.' He spoke as calmly as if he'd noticed nothing, but his chest was heaving with each breath.

Guilt flashed through her, seeing what she'd done to him. 'I—I didn't mean to…' she groaned, feeling like a complete dork. 'I mean…'

'I know you didn't mean that,' he said gently enough, but he'd turned from her, hiding the in- evitable male reaction to even accidental sensual talk. 'Let's get her inside. She looks like she's ready for a nap.'

Anna saw that the baby was indeed yawning, but her sparkling eyes still followed every animal movement that caught her attention. 'Okay, let's go,' she said, relieved he hadn't—

'But…' His eyes twinkled as he added, 'But if you decide you *did* mean it, now or any time at all, I'll be the happiest bloke in the Kimberleys.'

Blushing furiously, heart pumping with anticipation, Anna swung the baby up into her arms, put up the umbrella and ran into the rain before she could say anything stupid, like *Yes please*, or do something really dumb, like kiss him…

Shielding Melanie with the umbrella, she let herself get drenched as she ran: the outback equivalent of a cold shower and, boy, did she need it.

That night, after Melanie had been played and danced with to her little heart's content, fed, burped, changed and put to bed, Anna sat on her grandmother's old rocker on the front porch. She was stitching one of the patterns he'd bought her: a wild rose bush growing inside a forest.

She looked content. She looked beautiful.

Inside the living room, Jared sat on the sofa, sorting out the colours of thread she didn't yet need, and waited for her to say the words, that she'd changed her mind and she wanted him to take her to bed…

But she hadn't. She'd asked him to sit beside her as he'd sorted threads for her, but she'd mucked out the stables all afternoon with him, cooked dinner, and made conversation when he'd made some fumbling attempts to speak. She'd done nothing but give—and she'd made the offer to sit with her with such gentle distance he'd known she wanted to be alone.

So he watched her through the curtained window, filled with aching hunger. She was close enough to touch, to fill his inner darkness with her starlight, to give him sweetness and warmth in a world gone bleak and cold. But, fool that he'd been, he'd forged ahead with dreams when she had still been in love with him. He'd focussed on perfection, refusing to see truth, and he'd lost her. He'd lost her inside his dreams, left her behind, as she'd said. Though he could force her to stay by her promise, he no longer had the right to touch her, take her. He'd lost it all by himself, by sheer neglect.

What was he going to do? How could he live without her?

I love you...

He closed his eyes, bunched his fists. Oh, he had no doubt he could make her stay, even without reminding her of her promise. All he had to do was speak the three fatal words that would unleash the guilt and duty in her, as they had in his mother. Anna had never refused a duty in her life; he knew she wouldn't now. *I love you, Anna. Please stay and make my life right.*

But that was the issue: it was always about him, *his* life, *his* dreams. Anna had fed his dreams constantly from the day he'd kissed her in the haystack—she'd almost died trying to fulfil them, and still he'd pushed her away.

What kind of love was it that ignored the person

he loved, outside of his wants and needs? Like father, like son: he had no idea how to love. He was as destructive as his father.

He wouldn't hurt her again. It was time to give back—and if peace from his pursuit, and adopting Melanie was all Anna wanted from him, she could have them.

The phone rang at that moment. He greeted the caller absently as he tried to sort out grass green from forest green—which shade was this? He had no idea—

'Mr West? Hi, it's Rosie Foster…I'm so sorry…'

And then what she was saying, babbling really, sank in. His head snapped up, his gaze riveted on nothing as the world caved in on him.

No—it wasn't his world collapsing. *Anna's* world was about to cave in on her. Again.

'You want to talk to me?' His mother sounded subdued, but the sense of mild shock came down the line.

Jared had to release the jaw he'd clenched since first hearing his mother's voice, realising he'd been the one to call her. Conversation with her had been this hard since the day his mother had dumped him on Bryce like a bag of garbage. And to do this, asking for her help, was like drawing his own blood, cutting his throat; but he had no idea what else to do.

'Yes.'

'You haven't asked for anything from me in years.'

Since you threw away Dad's last letter with his words of love and apology for ruining our lives. You said his love was as bloody useless to you as the insurance he hadn't paid in months. 'Since I was fourteen,' he snapped.

Silence met his four-word attack. He took the phone into the glassed-in garden room at the end of the house, and closed the door. 'There are things you need to know. Anna's going to divorce me,' he said bluntly, 'and I don't know what to do to stop her.'

The silence this time was different. 'Oh, Jared,' his mother said at last, her voice soft with compassion. 'I was wondering when she'd leave.'

A few days before, he'd have demanded to know why Anna would ever want to leave him, leave their beloved home—but now he just waited, because he had to give his mother the full story, and she'd need time to digest every part of it.

'I don't think anyone can understand what she's been through,' she said at last.

'I tried to help. I lost Adam, too,' he growled, hating it that his mother seemed to understand immediately what it had taken him years to see. 'All the kids that died were mine, too!'

'But you didn't *fail*, son,' Pauline said very quietly. 'It wasn't your body that wasn't good enough, that killed those babies. Anna feels she failed you, and failed those children.'

Jared stilled, frozen over the phone. 'What? I never once thought that!'

His mother sighed. 'I wish your father were alive right now. I think he could help Anna as none of us can.'

Without warning he burst out, 'Don't. Don't you dare speak about my father!'

'It's time, Jared. If I don't, you'll lose Anna for good.'

The blunt words shocked him. 'Go on,' he said, hard and taut.

'Even though we inherited Mundabah in debt up to our ears, your dad felt like a failure. No matter what he tried, Mundabah sank deeper into debt. He borrowed from the bank to buy a thousand more sheep, and the Wet, the worst in fifty years, came and drowned out the enclosures; the poor things drowned in their own wool. It damaged the house and took the orchard, as well as the vegetables I'd planted.' She sounded tired and sad. 'Agistment of neighbouring horses, cattle and sheep was our sole method of keeping food on the table—that, and the fact that your dad was a good pilot. He got into crop dusting. That's why he taught you to fly. He planned on giving you your own business when you turned sixteen.'

The tenderness in her voice, as well as the tired acceptance, confused him still more. 'So why did he cheat the Eltons, selling their prize bull?'

'Desperation to look after us, to feed his children.' She sounded harder now. 'And they'd been robbing us blind for more than six years, demanding lower and lower agistment fees when their profits were rising. When your father found out the truth—that they'd been cheating him, even if it was done legally, on paper—well, he snapped. I know it's hard to see it, Jared, but your father was a good man, an honest man driven too hard.'

Jared gripped the phone so hard his fingers ached. He heard his next words dripping like icicles. 'You didn't see it that way when he was dead.'

Another sigh. 'You're a man now. You've had your share of grief. Have you never said anything you've regretted when you were in pain? I've never stopped loving your father. Why do you think it took me so long to marry again?'

And with the perspective of his stupidity with Anna, Jared heard the tears in his mother's voice, the regret that hadn't died in sixteen years, and he said, 'I'm sorry.' It came out rough and ungracious, but it was sincere.

'I know you are.' But she sounded as Anna had

before, so weary—*all I ever wanted was to try to make you happy*—and he wondered if he'd made it as hard for Anna as he obviously had for his mother, never letting either of them in. 'Richard Elton knew what he'd done to your father, to us all. All that money you sent him—he sent it to me. That was how I could afford to buy the house—and that's how we're setting up in Mundabah, with the sale price.'

'Can I ask what this has to do with Anna?' he asked cautiously.

'You know already,' his mother said, still sounding weary. 'You're so much your father's son, Jared—always full of plans, always trying new solutions. Yours work, I know that, but that's been as much a case of blind luck and inheriting a healthy property and a sackload of money as it is to your abilities.'

He frowned so hard his eyes slitted. He'd spent sixteen years trying to be someone else. 'When things are wrong, you have to try to fix it.' And heaven help him, he heard his father's echo coming down through the years...*I'll fix this, Pauline, I know what to do*...

'Is that the plan with Anna, Jared? What plans do you have to fix this problem—and does Anna know about them, appreciate them?'

The tart note in the questions surprised him because of the insight he hadn't expected, certainly not from his mother, who'd deserted him. 'At least I'm trying to fix it, not patching up my mistakes with inane words of love, like that makes it better!'

'Actually, it does make a lot of things better for a woman, son—or at least bearable.'

'What?' He shook his head to clear it. If he'd expected his mother's agreement on one thing, it had been on that. 'I heard you and Dad fighting, and him putting all the burdens on you. I heard what you said to him—and you said it the day he died. You said his love was useless, that at least insurance would feed us!'

'I was barely older than you are now when I said it. I'd just turned nineteen when I had you. I was thirty-three when your father died. Your father loved me, but he left me a widow at thirty-three with five children to feed, no job experience outside of farm work and bills and debts to pay. I had no way to look after you all. What would you have said? What would you have done that I didn't do?' Then, as he put himself in his mother's shoes for the first time, finally seeing why she'd given him to Bryce, and realising how many mistakes he'd made, she added, 'I was five years older than Anna is now. I know you've always blamed me for giving you to the Currans, no matter how happy you were there. Are you still blaming me, Jared? Do you blame Anna for feeling alone, unloved and a failure over Adam's death?'

With a fresh tide of shame washing through him, he realised that, though he hadn't blamed Anna for Adam's death, he had been blaming her for leaving him—until the past three days, when the bleeding shadows inside his wife's grief he'd been ignoring had finally come into the light. He heard the harsh truth behind his mother's gentle words—and he saw Anna through a woman's eyes.

Jared closed the eyes that had been blind for so long, said, 'Thank you.' He still found it hard to call her Mum after all these years separated, but today he felt as if he had a mother.

'I want you to look at your father's mistakes in life with a man's perspective. I know what he did seems rash, stupid, and ultimately it broke up our family—but without it we would have lost each other a year or two before we did... And I always knew he loved me, *needed* me.'

'You said it...made everything bearable?' Was that his voice, sounding so tentative? 'How could it? He lost everything. I remember hearing your fights. You said you couldn't work miracles for him, for us!'

'Can you, Jared? Can you pull off a miracle and give Anna the children she lost? And doesn't that make you feel angry that you're so helpless? And when you felt that helpless and stupid, didn't you say things you regretted later, or didn't say things you wished you had said?' she asked, still sounding drained, but the words hit him like a body blow. 'And even if you said or did nothing wrong, don't you think Anna still feels your anger, even when you hide it—and then she blames and hates herself a little more?'

He snapped, 'I never once said a word of blame or anger over Adam's death.'

'And you think silence makes it all right? You think she can't feel it?' A soft, pitying laugh came down the line, and he gave a start. 'My poor Jared, for all your success, you still know nothing about what women want. For all his mistakes, your father knew what it takes to make a woman happy. He knew how to make me feel needed, important— and he made sure I knew I was loved. Why do you think it took me fifteen years to find another man? Why do you think, despite all the hardships we suffered, I never once thought of leaving him?'

Jared's head was spinning; he felt hollowed out, scraped clean of all his life's sureties and pretensions. For the first time in the years since he'd come to Jarndirri, he felt truly humble. 'Tell me how to do that…Mum?'

She didn't mention him calling her Mum for the first time in years; he hadn't called her anything, and only now he wondered if he'd made her feel like nothing. 'There's something else,

isn't there?' she asked, and he could almost
envision that shrewd little frown on her face when
she'd seen or heard a nuance he'd been trying to
hide from her. 'Something's happened.'

'Yes, it has.' He looked around, checking to
see if Anna had come in, and then he told his
mother about the past few days—and about
Rosie's call tonight.

*You have no choice, Jared. You have to tell her
now, tonight.*

Half an hour after hanging up from his mother,
Jared watched Anna through the window, no
longer thinking about his pain, his need or the
promise she'd no longer have to keep; it was all
about her. Filled with aching love and helpless
pity, he closed his eyes, threw up a brief prayer
for help, and walked through the screen door.

As Anna pulled the thread through on the deep
scarlet heart of the rosebud on her stitchery, she
smiled and hummed a little. Though she'd been
alone most of the night, she felt peaceful. The
drumming rain on the tin roof had kept her
company, and she'd spent an evening without any
ghosts visiting her. The creative outlet had filled
her. She hadn't realised how much she'd missed
it—and she'd never *had* to miss it. One word to
Jared, and he'd have—

No. I could always have bought this myself, ordered art supplies and set up a room for myself. Even if Jared didn't understand, he'd have accepted it.

I could have done this any time the past five months without interference, she acknowledged to herself. *I was waiting for permission, just like I always have.*

Strange that an evening's sewing had made a woman of her. She'd waited all those years for the catalyst, the conversation, the acknowledgement from others of who and what she was—but the strength had had to come from inside her. Deep down it had been there all along.

'Anna.'

Smiling, ready for company, she pushed the needle through a hole in the folded material to hold it in place, and looked up. 'Hi. What have you—?' Then something inside went still and cold at the look in his eyes. The compassion, the fear—the desperate resolution. 'What is it?'

'I don't know any way to soften this.' Those sky-wet eyes, haunted, so unsure.

An odd sense of fatal calm touched her, like frost on young leaves, turning them brown and unfeeling. 'Then don't. Just say it now.'

He came to her, knelt at her feet, and laid his hands over hers. 'Rosie called.'

There it was: fate coming full circle. 'She wants

Melanie back, doesn't she?' she asked through lips that felt numb.

He bent his head, kissed the knuckles white from curled fingers. 'Maggie found out what's going on, and she called Rosie. She's offered to take Melanie, to move to Perth with her so Rosie can finish university and have her child.'

Funny, though he was kissing her hands between his words, she felt as if he'd landed body blows: she felt bruised and battered, without breath. 'Why did she change her mind?' she managed to say, wheezing it.

'I gather she thought Rosie would change her mind. Talking to Rosie made her see how much she loves Melanie, enough to be a single mother—alone, without Maggie's help, if need be.'

'I see.' She closed her eyes. She had to hand back her precious girl, leaving her with no child to love, an empty future...but hadn't part of her expected this all along? She'd always known how much Rosie loved Melanie. She'd been preparing for it, deep down, even as she'd allowed herself a tiny kernel of hope.

And now, facing the inevitable, there was choice: the slippery path of self-pity or the hard climb of strength. She'd been right yesterday: motherhood, to have a baby to love, was worth any sacrifice. *Any* sacrifice. She'd learned that the past few days. And that baby smile, those sweet chubby limbs, had helped put a healing scab on her endless wound.

The woman Anna had become tonight made the choice with a clean conscience.

After a minute or two of silence—or maybe half an hour—Jared said quietly, 'Rosie's half-hysterical with guilt, Anna. She's so sorry she's put you through this.'

Another minute, another half-hour, she nodded. 'It's all right—I always thought this would happen once she had treatment. Where's the number?' Wordlessly Jared pushed a piece of paper into her hand. Dry-eyed, legs steady, she got to her feet. 'Excuse me, please. I need to call her. Poor darling, she must be suffering so much,' she whispered. She felt a tiny dart of hard crystal touching her heart, cold, so cold. She moved past Jared to the door.

'Anna—Anna, I'm so sorry…'

Was that Jared's voice, tough, strong, in-control Jared, pleading? Some emotion touched her then, and she looked back over her shoulder. 'I don't blame you for this. I don't blame Rosie, or even Maggie. In fact, I think Rosie saved me. By giving me Melanie, she helped me come back to life.' A phantom's smile passed her lips. 'And let's be grateful you'll only have one court date to face. You don't have to commit perjury for me.'

She walked inside without looking back.

CHAPTER ELEVEN

IT WAS four a.m., but Jared still paced the verandah furthest from the room Anna was sharing with Melanie for the last time. There was no way he could sleep tonight. He had to stay awake in case Anna awoke and—

No, he thought wearily, *she won't come to me. She won't need me. She has Sapphie and Lea now, if she wants to talk.*

The woman he'd seen tonight left him in awe. She'd called Rosie, and asked simply, 'How are you, Rosie? You must be missing your baby.' She'd agreed that Bill could come by plane and take Melanie the next day—today. Rosie wanted Anna to come with the baby, but Anna said it was best if she didn't. Rosie thanked her for caring for her daughter from the heart. Anna said with tender warmth that she was welcome, that she'd always known Rosie couldn't leave Melanie behind.

And through it all, Anna spoke with such dignity and strength Jared was amazed. He called

Lea and Sapphie and asked them to comfort her, and she spoke to them, too. Expecting her to break down, he'd been lost in the undefeated power of Anna's giving, loving heart.

Anna was back, the Anna he adored—but she wasn't his any more. She was her own woman.

Lea and Sapphie arrived at Jarndirri around midnight, so close together it was as if they'd caught the same flight. Holding a sleepy Molly on her lap, Anna told them the whole story with a quiet dignity that left Jared shattered and speechless.

When Lea and Sapphie came to her, holding her from each side, she said simply, 'Girls, I'm not lying to you. I'll get through this. Melanie was a gift from God for as long as it lasted. She… made me want to live again.' And with a gulp that gave her away, she cried quietly in their loving arms.

Lea and Sapphie gave her the right kind of love, one that didn't say '*Don't go there*'.

How could he ever have blamed Anna for leaving him? He'd been the one to destroy their marriage, ruin her faith in him. He'd almost killed her with his demands.

No wonder she wouldn't cry for him. No wonder she didn't need him. Lea and Sapphie were just there for her, no conditions, no making their lives right at Anna's expense. They knew how to love.

He knew now, too. He just wished he'd known before it was too late.

Then Anna looked at the sleeping Molly and smiled, with an inner serenity that couldn't be faked. 'I'm sorry I avoided her—I should never have avoided you both, Lea. I thought it would be too painful, seeing the reminders of what I can never have, my own child. Seeing Molly now, I know she's a true blessing in my life—as you both are.' She smiled mistily at Lea and Sapphie. 'Thank you for putting up with me all this time until I came to my senses. I couldn't ask for better friends, more loving sisters. If you ever need anything, either of you, just ask, and it's yours. Right, Jared?'

Jared felt a rush of love as he nodded. How like Anna to include him, to keep him in the family promise, even as she was leaving him. 'Anything you two or Molly need, it's yours,' he said gruffly, his throat thick. Though he had nieces and nephews from Sam and Dale, Molly was special. 'You know that. We're family.'

And he ached at the word, finally understanding its meaning. All this time, all these years, he'd focussed on having a family all his own, to create a new, unbreakable circle—and he'd had it all along. He'd looked at children, his and Anna's, as a way of going forward and leaving the past behind—but he'd already moved on without knowing. And the parts of his past that had kept coming back to haunt him no longer troubled him. His dad had been a good man who'd made mistakes in life, just as he, Jared, had done. His dad had committed the crime of trusting too much, and failing the family he'd loved—and he, Jared, had done that too.

Despite his mistakes, his father was a man dearly loved by his family, years after his death.

Jared West was his father's son, and that was all right.

'Can't sleep either?'

The soft voice seemed to spin right out of his dreams and memories. Slowly he turned and, like a miracle, she was there, sweet and rumpled, barefoot and in a pink nightie. Pale, with dark rings under her eyes, she was still so beautiful to him he gulped. 'No.' Why, *why* couldn't he say what was in his heart, or give her the comfort he desperately ached to?

She stood in the doorway to the living room, the light from the kitchen framing her from behind. An empty-armed Madonna of Raphael's imagination, and it was physical pain to see her there, so lovely, so strong and yet so lonely. He yearned to touch her, to give something to take away the leaden ball in her heart.

Unable to help it, he began walking to her,

wishing he knew what to say or do to make it right, but as his mother had said, he was helpless. He stopped two feet short of touching her, the lost beauty in her face cutting his soul. 'I wish I could do something…'

A tiny, affectionate smile curved her mouth. 'It's okay, Jared. I don't need you to wave any magic wands. I'm okay.'

'I know you are,' he replied hoarsely. She was a woman now, strong enough to handle her suffering without his miraculous offerings to make it better. 'But I still want to.'

A humourless laugh, nearly silent, came from her, without the adorable donkey-braying at the end. 'Of course you do. You wouldn't be Jared if you didn't.'

'I'd do anything to make this go away, so you could have Melanie,' he blurted, and winced when she whitened at the name. 'I'm sorry, Anna, so damned sorry…'

A tiny shake of her head dried the words on his tongue. Stupid, inane words because he'd hit that wall of human limitation. There was nothing he could do.

'Melanie's well, and has a family to go home to. I'll even be able to see her sometimes, watch her grow up. I'll be her aunty Anna.' Anna closed her eyes, drew in a breath through her open mouth. She wetted her lips with her tongue.

'There's far worse suffering in the world than that. I can go on. I'll survive.'

He heard the farewell in what she hadn't said, and agony sliced through him. 'I know.' Now, the only thing he could do for her was set her free without guilt, and he'd do it if it killed him. 'But if you ever need anything from me—anything— I'll be here. Always.'

Wetness spiked her lashes. 'I know,' she whispered.

He saw her swallow, and hunger to take away the pain hit him like a surging river tide, taking him over.

'I know I have no right to ask this of you…'

'Ask,' he said hoarsely, palms and fingers straining to her, wanting to give something, anything, no matter what it cost him.

Her lashes lifted, spiky with tears, and she looked at him in mute longing. *Help me.* And she took one step, another.

Hands cradled her face, she was here, she was here—and he lowered his face, every moment anguish and beauty. He tasted her tears on his lips as he kissed her, felt her hands on his skin. Understood that this was less the familiar hunger than need for human contact…she needed *him.*

He carried her to the bedroom for what he knew would be the last time.

Afterwards, he held her in his arms, not letting

her go for a moment. He knew anything he said would be wrong, so he held her and waited.

'I held Melanie while she slept,' she whispered at last, caressing him with so much tender yearning, something splintered in him. 'I've been so jealous of Lea, so resentful. Wanting her life—but nobody's life is perfect.'

There were no words. He held her close, kissing her forehead, her eyes, her hair.

'What is it with us Curran women?' she whispered.

Though he knew what she meant, he murmured, 'I know…both so unforgettable.'

She looked up with a watery smile at that, but her eyes were shadowed in the night. 'Come with me into Adam's room?'

Anna hadn't been in there since the day they'd buried him. He'd been in a hundred times, seeing in the emptiness all they ought to have. It always gave him renewed determination to find a way to give Anna the babies she craved. But she'd closed the door that day, closing the door on their marriage, as he now knew, and she'd never gone in again. She'd begun leaving him that day, even though she'd stayed another seven months.

'Of course,' he said quietly.

They dressed and walked hand in hand to the little room next door to theirs—the door she'd refused to even look at as she'd passed.

'It looks so empty,' she said softly, seeing the cradle gone, the baby bath and changing table—all the things he'd given to the Lowes. The only things left here were the rocking chair she'd put in to feed their son, the blue paint on the walls and the hanging mobile where the cradle should have been. It bobbed in the tiny breeze created by the door's opening, painted in bright colours by a loving hand of the expectant mother.

The betrayal of what he'd done hit him in that moment, weeks too late.

But Anna squeezed his hand. 'I thought I'd feel anger—but no. It's good you gave it all away to someone who needed it, Jared. Hanging onto what's gone is useless.' She leaned on his shoulder. 'You were wiser than me.'

He shook his head. 'I did it in anger, Anna. You were giving up on me, on what I wanted, so I gave away what you created.'

'We all do things we regret.' A tiny breath that wasn't quite a sigh; she turned into his arms. 'Whatever happens, I'm glad for this week here. Part of me will always be on Jarndirri—and no matter where I am, part of me will always love you, Jared.'

No rush of exaltation; no bolting to take advantage of her love just to make his life right. Finally, he knew what love was—and here, in her arms, in the room of the son who'd never lived, on the last night he'd ever have with her, Jared knew what he had to do.

'My father killed himself when I was fourteen. He'd lost everything. He was going to be arrested on fraud charges. Rather than face it, he hanged himself in the barn—and I found him.'

He was amazed to hear his voice so steady. Anna didn't gasp or jerk back, but held him close, her head resting on his heart, sharing his inner darkness, taking half of it inside her and giving him healing in return. Funny how, when he'd always thought her the gentle one unable to bear his burdens and secrets, in fact she could handle all life hammered on her, and she only became stronger, more beautiful of heart and soul.

He told the story simply, without the blame that had weighed him down for so long. Finally he talked of the memory that came to his eyes day and night…the face as black as coal, the swinging feet he'd seen from outside the barn…

His stupid question: *Dad, what are you doing up there?*

Anna held him in silence, letting him talk it all out—and when he was done, though she still didn't speak, she kissed the skin covering his heart, and he felt as if she'd washed the blackness out of his soul. He felt cleansed, his secret shared, and she still loved him.

And she was still leaving.

She led him back to the bedroom, but they didn't make love. Wearing their nightclothes, they held each other, waiting for the dawn that would bring the end.

He'd given her one secret—and it wasn't enough. He knew that now. He'd been the keeper of Curran secrets for too many years, keeping them from Anna from a misplaced belief that he'd needed to shelter her, that she couldn't stand the strain. He knew better now.

'When you leave, keep Sapphie in mind, too,' he said quietly, playing with her hair. 'She's twenty-five next week—and she'll need a friend.'

Anna frowned up at him, but didn't ask—and he realised she knew him far better than she believed. 'Your father's will left Sapphie a special piece of information for her to receive on her twenty-fifth birthday.' And he told her the secret he'd been hiding for years, the bequest that could destroy Sapphie. 'When your mum was dying, your dad turned to Dana, her mother, for comfort. Sapphie's your half-sister.'

Now Anna did gasp. She gave her opinion on her father in a few pithy words. 'Lea knows, doesn't she? Lea somehow found out about them. That's why she hated him.'

Jared nodded. 'She saw them together…and she wouldn't hate him so much if she didn't love him more,' he said quietly, understanding that more than Anna ever could. Her conflict with her father had never been as deep-seated as Lea's—or his own—or with such cause.

Anna looked into his eyes for a long moment. 'That's the bond between you and Lea. You found your father's body—and she saw my father cheating on my mother. It was never sensual, or even that you were closer to her than me. You both knew how it felt. I didn't.'

In deep relief, knowing she knew at last without his having to betray Lea, he nodded.

She held him close, and the peace of heart and soul that was Anna slipped inside him, the snuggly blanket of love that was his consolation in a world dark and blank without her. 'And he put this on you? How long have you known about Sapphie?'

He shrugged. 'He told me a few weeks before he died.' He hesitated, but this, their last night together, wasn't the time to leave anything unsaid. 'But I wasn't surprised.' He smiled wryly. 'Even though she looks like Dana, she's always been like a bridge between you and Lea—and she *gets* you both, the way only family does.'

Anna only nodded. 'I'd ask why neither you nor Lea ever thought to tell me, but I think I understand now.' Her smile was wry, self-deprecating, but without anger or blame. 'Is there anything else about my life I need to know?'

'Only that Sapphie will need you and Lea both, I think, when she finds out. How Lea felt about your dad and why is her story to tell. You should talk to her, Anna. There's a lot about her life you do need to know. She really loves you—probably more than she knows.'

'I know that now.' A slow nod. 'Thank you, Jared.' She didn't have to ask to stay the night with him—they both knew she would. And he knew that, when the sun rose, it was over. The bags she hadn't fully unpacked would stand by the door by the afternoon.

There couldn't be a worse time to say *I love you*. Even if his mother was right and it made things bearable for a woman, made her want to stay, he knew if he started he wouldn't stop; he'd blurt out everything struggling to burst from his heart. Knowing that he'd rather live with her than have a dozen sons with another woman could only make Anna feel guilty now, when it was far too late, and all she wanted was peace and freedom.

All he could do was let her go, wish her happiness. Maybe one day he'd even wish she could find love again, with a better man—but not now. Not now.

So he kissed her and held her, giving her the choice; and when sweet caring turned to slow passion, it was right, it was beautiful. It was farewell.

* * *

The next afternoon, Anna hovered by the door of the plane as Bill strapped Melanie into a travelling seat. 'Don't forget to give her a bottle or rusk if she cries. She can't make her ears pop,' she said for at least the fourth time. 'And she'll need a nappy change.'

Bill flicked her a glance filled with compassion and caring. One of four guys who'd asked her out during her time in Broome, he'd been the only one she'd hesitated over before saying no. He was a good man. 'I'll take good care of her, Anna. I promise you.' He chucked Melanie under the chin. 'We'll have a great time, won't we?'

Melanie kicked her feet out, played with her fingers, gurgled and smiled at the young cop as he climbed into the plane. Bill had offered her a seat in the plane, but she'd shaken her head.

It had to be now, quick and clean, like an amputation, while she had Lea and Sapphie and Jared to help her let go, or she'd never let go. She'd packed a card in Melanie's bag with her contact details. On the back she'd written simply, *If you ever need anything, Rosie, Maggie, please call me. With love from Melanie's Aunty Anna.*

Bill turned to the pilot, and said curtly, 'Let's go.' He flung a quick glance at Jared standing silently behind her. Then he gave Anna one last, serious look, tried to smile and failed, nodded and pulled the door shut.

Anna looked at her sweet baby girl for the last

time. Her heart felt like an equation unsolved, full of fractured pieces, but still she didn't cry.

The momentary break in the weather, allowing Melanie to stay dry as Anna had carried her from the house to the hangar, ended in a hard downpour as the plane exited the hangar, heading for the runway. It seemed appropriate.

Don't do it, don't run after her. You can't change anything.

She'd done the right thing. She'd been mother-less most of her life. Melanie deserved a real family, with her real mother.

She stood in the hangar as the four-seater Cessna picked up speed and slowly lifted into the air. It disappeared into a dark grey curtain long before it reached the clouds.

'You okay, Aunty Anna?'

A lump filled her throat. Without any right to her love after the past year, Molly still gave it un-stintingly, and Anna knew it was because Lea had kept the love alive. 'I'm sad, baby. Can I have a special Molly-hug?' she whispered, lifting her niece into her arms.

Molly wrapped her little body around Anna in a monkey-cling. 'I lub you, Aunty Anna.' It came out *Aunnyanna*.

'I love you too, Molly,' she choked, and turned her face to Lea in silent thanks for flying through the night to give her what she needed, when she needed it: the unconditional love of her sweet Molly. She smiled at Sapphie. They'd both flown through the night in the Wet to come to her. She couldn't ask for better friends, sisters.

She was blessed.

A moment later, Lea said gruffly, 'Molly, you need your nap.' She took her daughter from Anna's arms and, covering her daughter with a rain poncho, ran for the house.

As usual, Sapphie didn't have to say it, didn't have to ask. She knew talking about it now would only make her cry, so she didn't. She said quietly, 'I'll make dinner,' kissed Anna's cheek and ran for the house in Lea's wake.

They knew she was leaving.

Jared's warm hand caressed her shoulder in silent support. Anna's mouth quirked in a wry acknowledgement of the strangeness of life. He was giving her all she'd asked for, all she'd wanted—almost. Once, it would have been enough to make her stay. But it was too late—too late to stay, either at Jarndirri, or with Jared.

All that was familiar and loved was here. Ahead lay an uncertain future. But she knew she had to go, or live with a lifetime of regret. And she had to go today. A quick, clean break from all she'd hoped for, an amputation of heart and spirit.

'Are your bags packed?' he asked quietly,

walking into her mind with the uncanny accuracy he'd always had with her, and he wasn't hiding from it or trying to change her mind.

She nodded, unable to look at him.

'You want to go now, don't you?'

Again she nodded. In a smaller plane than the police one, she'd be an hour behind them by the time she left—and Melanie would be on her way to Perth with Maggie. She could fly herself home, and Ollie, one of Jared's most trusted employees, would be able to fly it home on his way back from holiday.

Her hands shook. For the second time she was losing a baby and a marriage in a day—but this time there was no self-pity. At last, she knew she could move on, say goodbye.

'I'll get the plane ready.' Jared's voice was rough, jerky. Filled with unashamed pain.

'Thank you,' she choked. 'Jared…'

'Get your things.' So curt, that empty well scraped dry again—but it no longer fooled her. She knew he cared, that if she said the word she could stay for ever—but he had no idea what life with her would be like. Living a lifetime with a woman who couldn't give him his one soul-deep craving, who couldn't bear to live with him in the home of his heart…

There were regrets no matter what choices she made today—but at least she could set him free to find life and love and a family. And if she'd never stop loving him, that was her problem. She had to love him enough to let him go.

She walked into the pounding rain without looking back.

Jared packed her bags into the tiny cargo hold at the back, strapping them down, then climbed out, pushed the door shut and faced her. 'The plane's full of fuel.'

Anna looked up at the sky, gauging. 'The weather forecast said there should be just rain and no electrical activity until I reach Broome. I can fly that far.' She smiled at him, scared yet serene. 'Thank goodness for specially modified wheels for the Wet.'

He shuddered, and kept his fears and longings to himself, kept his mouth shut by brute force. *I love you. Please stay with me.*

He couldn't leave, and she couldn't stay.

'Safe trip,' he managed to grate out. It didn't sound like his voice. 'Call me when you get back, let me know you're okay.'

'I will.' Her eyes wandered over his face. 'I might think about heading to Perth or maybe Sydney one day. I want to apply for a teaching position.'

Didn't she remember how she'd hated even the small city of Perth when she'd been at boarding school, how her spirit had felt starved until she'd come home to Jarndirri? How could she be thinking of a city of over five million—?

I starved her of affection and ignored her dreams, until Jarndirri was no longer home to her. I've lost the right to remind her.

'Well, I guess I should go.' She sounded sad, yet certain. She had no doubts—and his heart, already splintered, broke in silence.

He couldn't help it, couldn't stop it. He stepped into her, grabbed her face in his hands and kissed her over and over, face, hair, lips. 'I'll be here.'

Her eyes closed, her lashes turned spiky with wetness. 'I know,' she whispered, and broke away from him. So much love, too much loss. How could she stay?

The rain pounded on the roof of the hangar as she climbed into the cockpit and closed the door. The plane fired up and began moving—out of the hangar, down the runway; it began picking up speed—

Something in him snapped; for the first time in his life he saw the choice clearly, and he made it without doubt or regret. He ran out and after the plane, tripped and landed on his knees in four-inch-deep water, scrambled up and kept running. 'Anna! Anna, wait!' he yelled. 'Anna! *Anna!*'

Water sluiced all over him as she slowed the Cessna. The pilot's door flew open; from beneath the wing she peered at him. 'What is it?' she yelled over the hard drumming rain.

He felt like a drenched cat and looked worse, but didn't care. He ran to her, stood in the driving rain and shouted, 'I only barely survived losing Adam. I don't think I'll survive losing you. Come back to me, Anna, come back.'

Her bottom lip sucked in; finally she lost her hard-fought control, and tears fell. 'I *can't*,' she cried. 'I can't be here any more. Please don't ask me to stay here. Not after today, not after losing Melanie. And you love Jarndirri—and you want children—'

Desperate to make her understand, he lifted a hand to stop her. 'I can handle leaving Jarndirri. I can live without kids. But I can't stand another day, another hour without you. Come back to *me*, Anna. Come back to *me*.' He hoped to God all he wasn't saying was clear for her to see in his eyes. *I love you, I adore you, please, please take me back and give me a chance.*

Her gaze remained steady on his face as he laid bare his love without words. He could see her mind racing. Then her eyes grew wide, firm with resolve. She lifted her chin and said, 'The door's open, Jared. Get in.'

There was no compromise. She was giving him only one choice: life without Jarndirri, or life without her. He looked around the place he'd loved for so long, the only life he'd wanted—

until now. Yes, an uncertain future lay ahead with Anna, in unfamiliar territory, without full control of his life and destiny—but if he let her go now, he faced certain loneliness without her, a life without love. He was pretty sure he could survive without Jarndirri, without children if he had to—but he *knew* life without Anna was unbearable. 'Can I pack a bag first?'

Her eyes, glittering with tears, lit and shone. She bit her lip, and slowly laughed, with that cute little snort he loved. 'Sure. I can wait five minutes.'

He was back in four, running for the plane in case she changed her mind. He slipped and fell in the water again, totally soaked and wetting his case; but before he could scramble to his feet, she was out of the plane, and tender hands were helping him up. He smiled at her, touched her face with a fingertip. 'Lea and Sapphie said they're happy to stay and care for the animals until the men are back. Ollie can run the place as station manager. He's more than capable.'

She stood before him, her eyes glowing and uncertain as rain ran like a waterfall down her face. 'Jared, are you sure?'

His heart nearly bursting with all he'd kept locked in so long, he still didn't know how to say it. Shaking, he took one of her hands in his, and placed it on his heart. His eyes fixed on hers, pleading in silence for her to understand.

Her eyes darkened, filled with the love she'd believed was gone and he'd feared was dead. She leaned into him, and kissed his chest. 'If you ever change your mind—'

His beautiful Anna—*his beloved wife*—still setting such a low value on herself, believing herself less important to him than a million hectares. He buried his face in her hair. 'I'm thanking God you changed yours,' he mumbled. 'I'm praying you never change it back.'

'But…what will you do in the city, if we go there?'

'I don't care what job I do. As for the rest, I'll do whatever it takes to make you happy with me,' he said hoarsely.

She looked up at him, her soft doe's eyes filled with joy. 'I love you, Jared,' she mumbled, and drew him down to her for a long kiss, sweet, ready passion and pure happiness.

It moved him to the soul. He'd come so close to losing everything…and now he *had* everything that truly mattered in life. And in that kiss Jared blessed God, his mother's wisdom and second chances.

EPILOGUE

Mumbai, India, three years later

'SO THAT is finally everything, Mr and Mrs West. Congratulations on the adoption of your daughters Aisha and Maya. May your family life in Australia be blessed and filled with beauty.'

The rotund Indian man beamed as he shook hands with Jared and bowed to Anna, whose hands were full with two little girls, one clinging to each of her hands, eighteen-month-old and three-year-old orphaned sisters. Their parents had died within weeks of each other and Aisha and Maya had needed a home and family as much as she and Jared needed children to love.

Her heart was full at last. The long months of waiting for the formal adoption to go through had been worth every moment. They'd spent the time getting to know Aisha and Maya, learning Hindi and teaching the girls basic

English. She was totally besotted, as was Jared. Beautiful girls both, they called her Mami and Jared Papi.

And to think that two years ago she couldn't have imagined this blessing in her life...

She bowed her head in return. '*Namaste*,' she said softly. 'Thank you for helping to bring this joy to our lives.'

Jared swung Aisha up into his arms, she held little Maya, and they walked out of the office, parents at last. They were staying another week in India, in the apartment they'd taken while the adoption went through.

'Mami, where are we going?' Aisha asked in Hindi as Jared carried her into the street pulsing with humid sunshine.

'We're going home, Aisha.' They'd been taking the girls to the apartment on a daily basis, to get them used to the place, and to a small family unit.

'Straya?' Aisha asked, stumbling over the long word. They'd been teaching the girls where home was, to get them used to the coming change.

Jared laughed. 'Yes, Australia, Aisha...and we go there next week. We have pictures of Australia to show you when we get home. Aunty Sapphie sent you pictures of her home—and Aunty Lea sent pictures of Molly waving to you.'

'We go see Aunty Lea, Aunty Sapphie and Molly,' Aisha parroted wisely, and Anna and Jared laughed. Maya was chattering in baby-talk Hindi, with a little arm around Anna's neck.

'And the rest of the family,' Jared added. 'Don't forget your nanna Pauline and grandpa Mikey, and all your other aunts, uncles and cousins.'

'Yes, Papi. And when do we go on the little ride, and the big ride?' Aisha asked eagerly, her massive dark eyes alight with fun. Jared wanted to take them up in a small plane to help them acclimatise to cabin pressure before putting them on a 747 for Perth next week, where their new lives would begin.

'The little ride is tomorrow, and the big one next week.' Jared tweaked her nose, and Aisha shrieked with laughter.

That night, in bed, Jared and Anna lay entwined, her head on his chest, talking softly. The girls' door was open, their first night in a new place.

'Happy?' he murmured, kissing her hair.

'How could I not be?' She smiled up at him. 'I have you, and two beautiful daughters. We're a family.'

From the moment he'd climbed in the plane, Jared had gone wherever she'd wanted without question. He'd taken a job as a horse trainer for the racing industry in Perth—his reputation had ensured the big noises in the industry came to him with lucrative offers—while Anna had applied for teaching positions.

She'd found true joy, as well as hard work, when she'd accepted a position teaching challenged children, not just art but to sing and dance. In working with children who truly needed her, she'd found true peace in her soul. She'd come home to Jared every afternoon with some new story to laugh over or just to hold him as she'd shared something poignant, she always felt a new peace and happiness in her heart—and to his own surprise Jared found his new work exciting and fulfilling.

They worked hard at their new jobs with all their challenges; they worked hard at learning how to live in the city—and, hardest of all, they worked at their marriage. To Anna's surprise, Jared showed no sign of regret; and if he missed Jarndirri and his old life, he said simply that having Anna's love more than made up for his loss.

After two years Jared took her away to Bali for a holiday—he called it an anniversary of their new marriage. After two weeks of surfing, sailing and generally being spoiled thoroughly, Jared had tentatively brought up the question of adopting kids from poorer nations, orphans who truly needed a stable, loving home and parents who'd love them.

To her surprise, she was ready to hear it, ready to look at the websites he'd been quietly gathering in his spare time the past year.

After days of searching the net for adoption sites, they'd seen a picture of Maya and Aisha, tiny, sweet, big-eyed girls with smiling faces—and they knew they'd found their family at last. They'd applied to adopt them, and hopped on a flight to Mumbai before anyone else claimed the children they already saw as their daughters. Now they had their family. Life didn't get better than this.

'*Ti amo*,' Jared said softly in Italian, lifting her face to kiss her, soft and sensual.

'*Je t'aime*,' she replied in French, kissing him back…and they made love gently, quietly so they didn't wake the girls.

Some time in the first year in Perth he'd taken to saying *I love you* in other languages. She didn't question why he never said it in English; he'd tell her in his time and way, and he had. Now it was a prelude to love-play for them, coming up with new languages in which to say it—though for some reason saying it in Finnish had them rolling around with laughter instead of sensuality.

Afterwards, they lay together, drifting toward sleep. Then Anna said the words she'd been rehearsing for days, weeks. This was the right time. 'I'm ready to go home.'

'We will,' he replied, more than half-asleep. 'Just give the girls a few days to—'

'No, Jared,' she said softly, and kissed his chest. 'I mean, I'm ready to go home to Jarndirri.'

She felt him turn still for a few moments. 'Do you mean that? You're not just saying it for me?'

The repressed eagerness in his voice made her smile. 'No, I'm saying it for all of us. Jarndirri is a fantastic place to bring up kids. Aisha and Maya love animals. I think they'll take to it like ducks to water.' She smiled up at him. 'I'd like to invite Rosie and Melanie up, too. They can be cousins, as well.'

'But how do you feel about going back?' He lifted her face, his gaze searching hers.

'I have two healthy, happy children who need room to play and animals to love—and a husband who's proven *ehr liebt mich* more than any million hectares,' she added, smiling in impish fun at saying *he loves me* in German. 'I think Adam's memory will be sweet for us both now.' She drew a deep breath and lifted her chin. 'I'm ready to be a Curran woman again, to be the person I was always meant to be. I want to live the rest of my life on Jarndirri. I know that now.'

He lifted her up until they were face to face—and whatever he saw in her eyes made his light with joy. He mumbled through fervent kisses, 'Thank you, Anna, thank you—but if you change your mind…'

As he'd done three years ago when she'd used those words, she put his hand over her heart. Giving him the assurance he needed without words. 'We're going home.'

'No.' And he shook his head, smiling that slow half-smile she'd always loved. 'I'm already home, when I'm with you and our girls.'

* * * * *

Harlequin Intrigue top author Delores Fossen presents a brand-new series of breathtaking romantic suspense!
TEXAS MATERNITY: HOSTAGES
The first installment available May 2010:
THE BABY'S GUARDIAN

Shaw cursed and hooked his arm around Sabrina.

Despite the urgency that the deadly gunfire created, he tried to be careful with her, and he took the brunt of the fall when he pulled her to the ground. His shoulder hit hard, but he held on tight to his gun so that it wouldn't be jarred from his hand.

Shaw didn't stop there. He crawled over Sabrina, sheltering her pregnant belly with his body, and he came up ready to return fire.

This was obviously a situation he'd wanted to avoid at all cost. He didn't want his baby in the middle of a fight with these armed fugitives, but when they fired that shot, they'd left him no choice. Now, the trick was to get Sabrina safely out of there.

"Get down," someone on the SWAT team yelled from the roof of the adjacent building.

Shaw did. He dropped lower, covering Sabrina as best he could.

There was another shot, but this one came from a rifleman on the SWAT team. Shaw didn't look up, but he heard the sound of glass being blown apart.

The shots continued, all coming from his men, which meant it might be time to try to get Sabrina to better cover. Shaw glanced at the front of the building.

So that Sabrina's pregnant belly wouldn't be smashed against the ground, Shaw eased off her and moved her to a sitting position so that her back was against the brick wall. They were close. Too close. And face-to-face.

He found himself staring right into those sea-green eyes.

How will Shaw get Sabrina out?
Follow the daring rescue and the heartbreaking
aftermath in THE BABY'S GUARDIAN by
Delores Fossen,
available May 2010 from Harlequin Intrigue.

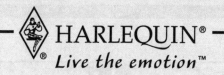

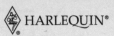

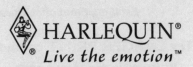

HARLEQUIN®
INTRIGUE®

BREATHTAKING ROMANTIC SUSPENSE

Shared dangers and passions lead to electrifying romance and heart-stopping suspense!

Every month, you'll meet six new heroes who are guaranteed to make your spine tingle and your pulse pound. With them you'll enter into the exciting world of Harlequin Intrigue— where your life is on the line and so is your heart!

THAT'S INTRIGUE— ROMANTIC SUSPENSE AT ITS BEST!

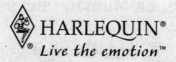

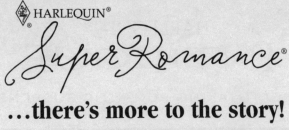
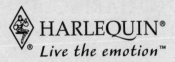

Harlequin® Historical
Historical Romantic Adventure!

*Imagine a time of chivalrous
knights and unconventional ladies,
roguish rakes and impetuous
heiresses, rugged cowboys
and spirited frontierswomen—
these rich and vivid tales will
capture your imagination!*

*Harlequin Historical . . .
they're too good to miss!*

HHDIR06

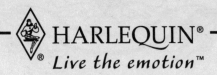

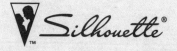